Pie Man

John Surowiecki

Southeast Missouri State University Press | 2017

Pie Man by John Surowiecki

Softcover: $18.00
ISBN: 978-0-9979262-4-8

First published in 2017 by
Southeast Missouri State University Press
One University Plaza, MS 2650
Cape Girardeau, MO 63701
www.semopress.com

Cover Design: Carrie M. Walker

Denise: This? This is for you.

Special thanks to early readers and supporters, Jon Andersen, Anne Flammang, Andy Levesque, and Jack Sawicki.

THADDEUS

1

I WAS CALLED TADEUSZ OR TADEK BY MY LATE wife and parents and am still called that today by my friend, Witold Marek, and other old-country acquaintances. I'm called Ted or Teddy or Thaddeus by my American friends and former coworkers at the Aircraft (I've been retired for a thousand years, it seems), Mr. Olszewski (pronounced *Ol-shev-ski* or *Ol-zoo-ski*) by my neighbors and Mr. O. by my son's former tutor and by the neighborhood youngsters.

My late wife, Agnes Olszewska, *née* Tencza (pronounced *Ten-cha*) was called Agnieszka (*Ag-nee-ehsh-ka*) by her family, sometimes by me and always by her closest friend, Danuta (whom she called Danka), and Mrs. Olszewska (*Ol-shev-ska* or *Ol-zoo-ska*) by our neighbors, the neighborhood boys and girls and her employees.

She was never called Mrs. O.

My parents, Adam and Lilka Olszewski, and Agnes's parents, Adam and Ania Tencza, came from the same town in Poland, but they were ashamed to say what that was because during the war the Germans had built a camp there and had turned the town's name into a synonym for suffering and misery and death.

The Pie Man, my son, was sometimes called The Hermit of Peru Street. His actual name was Adam Olszewski. When he was a boy he was known as Adam O. In his thirties he became known as Pie Man, a name he accepted without hesitation despite the fact that it was a misnomer and despite the heartbreak associated with it at the time.

2

AS CHILDREN AGNES AND I WERE PRACTICALLY brother and sister. In high school we became sweethearts and some people actually disapproved of our relationship because to them it seemed almost incestuous. Agnes and I grew up in Massachusetts within walking distance of each other on small, stubbornly productive farms. When the two Adams, my father and hers, came to this country, they worked in the local mills and foundries, while our mothers, Ania and Lilka, did whatever they could to make money: taking in laundry, mending clothes, cleaning houses. The couples lived in cramped, mold-ridden rooms and, like most of their neighbors, they barely spoke English and had only a vague notion that they had become living personifications of ignorance, squalor, and dimwittedness.

Eventually, the two Adams saved enough money to put a down payment on two failed and derelict farms that were, by a happy coincidence, adjoining properties. In time, they revived the neglected apple orchards, planted hundreds of trees, constructed greenhouses, rebuilt an ancient cider press, grew assorted vegetables and berries and turned over most of their mutual acreage to sweet yellow corn. At the end of every summer, the families combined their resources, selling their produce and gallon jugs of fresh cider at a roadside stand, a rickety old shack, really, located along the winding road that separated the two properties. The families also allowed folks to wander through their orchards, either on their own or accompanied by Agnes, filling bags with fruit so long as they paid for the privilege of doing so.

As a boy, I was what people called mechanically inclined, so it was no surprise to anyone that I went to trade school to study automobile mechanics. Like many of my fellow students, I enlisted in the army after Pearl Harbor. I spent most of the war in England where I was a mechanic in a motor pool outside London. I suppose I was in danger as much as anyone else, but in all honesty I had it pretty easy. I was not on the front lines. I was not shot at. I was not destined to be one of those young men I saw at the base hospital who were either broken, or frightened, or extravagantly stoic. Most of the time I spent under the hood of a jeep or half-track. Only now and then did I allow myself the pleasure of wandering the English countryside: it reminded me of the Massachusetts farmland I missed so much.

A few months after I returned home, Agnes and I were married. Before the war, I had every intention of working for my father and hers and eventually taking over, with Agnes, of course, the operation of the two farms. But when I came home, I wanted to make a living using my mechanical training. Anyway, the two Adams were still young men. They and their wives didn't really need Agnes and me: they had no problem taking care of the farm and business.

When I applied for work as a mechanic at a large Aircraft plant in Silverton, Connecticut, I was pretty much hired on the spot. We moved to Silverton a week later, renting a tiny apartment with bad pipes and decayed linoleum. At the Aircraft, I was the guy who readapted, repaired, and resuscitated the lathes and grinders and lift trucks and who knows what else in the plant. Three years later, I was promoted to master mechanic.

Of course, Agnes, being Agnes, refused to sit at home doing nothing and soon found a job as a cleaning woman at the Silverton Hotel, known in town as the Silverfish. There she met Danuta Jagelska who would quickly become her best friend. The work was demanding and demeaning and though Agnes didn't make much money, every penny she earned, plus a good deal of my salary, went directly into our savings.

With that money and some money from our parents (a gift not a loan) we were ready to buy a home of our own: a large gray house at 7 Peru Street in Silverton. We wanted nothing to do with banks or real estate agents or mortgages. Agnes got a little sick to her stomach when she learned how much in interest we were required to shell out to the bank over thirty years, so we paid in cash: eighty-six crisp hundred-dollar bills, which I carried to the closing in a paper bag.

Adam was born the very next week.

Two days later, we moved into our new home.

3

MY SON WAS BORN IN THE LATE AFTERNOON OF March 14, 1950. The trees were brown and lifeless; the grass, pitted by patches of snow, was hardly green at all; and mud was everywhere. It didn't seem right to Agnes that her beautiful baby was born when the world was at its least beautiful.

From that day on, Agnes's devotion to our son was intense and boundless. While I worked double shifts at the Aircraft (foolishly believing that the plant couldn't function without me), she took care of him. When he was a toddler, she took him to museums, libraries, and art galleries, places she'd never been to and thought herself unworthy of entering. She took him to the movies at local cinemas and on walks through the park on Peru Street, a block from our house. She took him to New York at Christmastime where they gawked at the shop windows and watched the skaters at Rockefeller Center. Never a good reader, she struggled through books on child rearing and child psychology and nutritional science, trying her best to be a loving modern mother.

She recorded on 8mm film the achievements of Adam's young life as if they would be of historical significance one day, an invaluable record of a great man's childhood. She usually tried for candid shots, but the whirring camera and bar of blinding lights always gave her away. She also took hundreds of snapshots during Adam's early years, but only rarely did she step in front of the lens. A significant loss, I think, because she was such an attractive woman. Her skin was as dark as coffee with a few drops of milk in it, her eyes were as black as coal, and her hair was even blacker. Most of the images we have of her are mistakes, a reflection in a window or a shadow on a wall—and always with the camera to her eye.

4

ONE DAY, WHEN ADAM WAS FOUR, HE TOLD US that the house, our house at 7 Peru Street, was alive. And not only was it alive, it was *him*. The house encased him, protected him, gave him form, gave him water, fed him, removed his waste, cooled him, warmed him, kept him dry. The house spoke to him as well and they spent hours talking to one another. He was the house, he said, but he had been given the shape of a boy. We wondered why Adam would think such a thing and concluded that maybe in his eyes the house was a kind of fortress. But the more we thought about it, the less sense that made. The world was no threat to Adam. In fact, he wasn't afraid of anything. He was a happy-go-lucky little man who was friendly and cheerful and full of boyish mischief.

Adam said the house liked me. He never said he, Adam, liked me. And he never said he *and* the house or he *as* the house liked me. All he ever said was the house liked me. Why? Because I took care of it. I maintained it. I added showers to the bathrooms, put in shelves, mended walls and windows, added a kitchen island ("just like at a restaurant," Agnes said) and replaced the wood-burning kitchen stove with a new gas model. Outside, I designed and dug up Agnes's vegetable and flower gardens, laid down cobblestone pathways, and in the corner of the property, planted a grove of white birches and fruit trees. At one point I noticed that Adam was very curious about my chores around the house. I thought he was studying me, learning from me, a son watching his father figure things out and break things down and put them together again; but then I realized that he was just keeping an eye on me, making sure I didn't do anything that would displease the house.

One thing was certain, the house wasn't a place where the laws of physics and mathematics prevailed. There were other forces at work that didn't run motors or push water through pipes or heat rooms, nameless forces that came and went without affecting anyone except Adam. The house was his brother or pal. It touched him, danced with him, played with him, caressed and petted him and spoke to him in a language of noises, creaks, and thuds from the floors and ceilings, rattles and shudders from the doors and windows, and clanks, clunks, hisses, whistles, toots, and bangs from the pipes and steam radiators. Adam soon learned to converse with the house and they spent hours talking to each other. About what? Childish things, I suppose: toys, games, comics, books, television shows. Sometimes Adam and the house giggled over some silly bit of news or else they shared whispered secrets or asides in a melodrama or opera. Sometimes Adam spent entire afternoons huddled in a corner of the parlor or kitchen singing songs in a stop-and-go fashion as if he were teaching the house the lyrics. One time, when Adam was daydreaming in the kitchen and not paying attention to what Agnes was telling him, she reprimanded him. "Do you think I'm talking to the wall?" she asked. That woke him up and made him laugh, because quite often he really did talk to the wall.

Another time Agnes and I saw him sitting on his bed, purring, his eyes closed in a kind of ecstasy, acting like a cat being stroked.

"Who is doing this to you?" Agnes asked.

Adam smiled. "The house," he said.

"You think the house is alive?" asked Agnes.

"Yes, it's alive."

"Is every house alive?"

"I don't know. I don't think so."

"Just this house."

"This house is alive."

"But how can this be, Adam? A cat or a dog is alive, Mrs. Chmura next door is alive, your father is alive, I'm alive, but a house, no. A house isn't a living thing, it's just a thing. It's made of brick and wood and metal. Are you made of brick and wood and metal?"

"No."

"That's right, you're made of flesh and blood and bone. That's what makes you alive like your papa and me and Mrs. Chmura. Is the house made of flesh and blood and bones?"

"No."

"Then how can it be alive?"

"It's alive. It's me," he said finally, looking away as if he were deeply ashamed of us, as if we had betrayed him. Agnes and I didn't know what to make of any of this. We had no idea what was happening to our son. We thought he might be going crazy before our very eyes. We thought of asking Dr. Cohen, our family physician, to examine Adam or put him through some kind of psychological examination, but we decided to wait, convincing ourselves that Adam's identification with the house might be innocent and harmless, the result of an overactive imagination. Still, we were worried sick about it. Mostly we were afraid that policemen would crash into our house and forcibly take him away, bring him to a hospital, and we would never see him again. People told us that sort of thing didn't happen in this day and age, but we didn't believe them. We were only a few years away from a war where millions of people were slaughtered and millions of families torn apart. And even then, and even in Connecticut, we had heard stories about people being sent to lunatic asylums by judges and officials. And this happened without recourse and without reason except that it was supposedly for someone's own good or the good of others. The thought of Adam being taken away terrified us. Agnes and I vowed we would do anything to keep that from happening.

5

AT FIVE, LITTLE ADAM HAD NO FEAR OF OTHERS, nor was he afraid to venture out into the world. He even had a best friend, Jake Glowac, a rough-and-tumble boy who often acted as his protector. But things began to change that spring, although gradually: a bowl of soup, my mother used to say, doesn't cool off all at once. More and more, it seemed, Adam preferred staying in to going out, spending his time reading or drawing in his room or watching movies and cartoons in the den. He even balked at going on our Sunday drives, his favorite activity, and only acquiesced when I, tired of arguing and cajoling, insisted. When Adam started school we didn't know what to expect.

Agnes, who was not religious, didn't want to send Adam to parochial school, but after Danuta and various neighbors warned her that the city schools were lax and unchallenging, and even academically suspect, she decided Adam might be better off going to St. Paul in Chains School, which was, after all, just a few blocks away from us on the corner of Olive and Canada Streets. On his first day of kindergarten, Adam bawled when Agnes left him in the nuns' care. Nearly all the other children cried as well, but they did so because they missed their parents. Adam cried because he knew he would have to spend an entire morning, hour after miserable hour, outside the hard gray skin of his house.

As time passed, Adam seemed to adjust to school. There was plenty of roughhousing and teasing to be sure, but it was harmless and Adam didn't seem to mind it. His classmates were fond of him, sharing jokes and toys with him, inviting him to their homes and to Saturday afternoon birthday parties. Most important, there was little mention of the house. We no longer found Adam talking to walls or being caressed by the house. At the dinner table Adam mostly talked about his classmates and teacher and asked again and again if he could get a bike for Christmas since some of his little pals were already experienced riders. We were hopeful these were all positive signs.

But by the time Adam entered the first grade, he was routinely making up reasons to stay home, no doubt because he was expected to be in class the entire day. All Agnes and I knew for sure was that the progress he had made in kindergarten and the summer that followed it had vanished. It had been a wonderful summer, idyllic almost, with plenty of day trips and Sunday drives, plus daily adventures with his friends as they biked up and down neighborhood streets (Santa did bring him a new blue Schwinn). But by September, he no longer wanted to play with his mates or ride his bike (it collected dust in my workroom), and when school began, Adam feigned illness so often that on several occasions Dr. Cohen refused to come out and see him, calling him "a big faker."

Adam didn't mind being in school once he got there: what he found disturbing was leaving the house. He told us that the best part of going to school was leaving school, walking up Olive Street and then down Bolivia Street, and then, at the corner of Bolivia and Peru, seeing his magnificent gray house and the brass "7" shining in the late-afternoon sun.

The thing was, we weren't really listening to him.

Our concern and focus was the school and not the house. We were worried about his studies and teacher and fellow students and it took us a while to realize that the house, our old nemesis, had returned and seemed to have an even stronger hold on Adam's psyche.

6

THAT YEAR, ADAM BEGAN TO DREAM THAT HE had actually, physically, become his house, a *House-Adam*, and he would stomp around the neighborhood, shingles and rain spouts and pieces of wood and plaster flying from his frame.

In some of those dreams, my son would tell me, the *House-Adam* destroyed the other, smaller houses and, in a language of floor creaks and radiator hisses, ridiculed its neighbors with scornful insults before reducing them to piles of rubble. Sometimes the *House-Adam* attacked the children who scrambled out of the fallen houses like so many cockroaches, crushing them with its sheer tonnage, ignoring their cries for mercy, watching a river form from their blood.

In some dreams, the *House-Adam*, ashamed at what it had done, at its baseness and disregard for life, wept until its wood rotted, its metal rusted, and its shingles were washed away.

7

IN THE EARLY MORNING OF ADAM'S SEVENTH birthday, the house refused to let him go outside its walls or, as Adam would later explain, leave its dominion. The sky was just turning light and Adam was on his way outside to see how much snow had fallen during the night. As he opened the kitchen door that led to the backyard (and, off to the right, my workshop), something, an invisible membrane of some sort, stopped him from crossing the threshold and threw his thin frame to the kitchen floor. Adam tried again and again to penetrate the barrier, only to be rebuffed each time. A few minutes later, Agnes and I, coming downstairs for breakfast, discovered our son spread-eagled on the kitchen floor, shaking, gasping for breath, and barely able to explain to us that the house was somehow preventing him from going into the backyard. Agnes immediately became suspicious and asked if he were playing tricks again in order to stay home from school, but Adam insisted he wasn't joking or pretending.

Without giving any warning, I scooped up Adam and carried him like a football over the threshold, but the instant we broke the plane between indoors and outdoors he began screaming. His throat contracted as if a hand were squeezing it shut. Blood gushed from his nose and he turned blue, nearly the blue, Agnes later said, of a milk of magnesia bottle. Then his body shook in the most hideous way, his arms and legs flailing and his face shifting and twisting into grotesque shapes. I tried to keep him still, but I couldn't. I didn't know what to do. I looked to Agnes for help, but she was already in the living room talking on the phone, desperately trying to get Dr. Cohen on the line.

When the doctor arrived an hour or so later, we tried to explain what happened. We must have sounded like a pair of idiots blabbering about doorway membranes and such. Adam was in his room and Dr. Cohen went upstairs to examine him. He returned after ten minutes and reported to us that Adam was perfectly healthy, physically speaking, which meant that he was either a very good actor and a bigger faker than any of us thought or that he was going through some kind of psychological episode. One way to determine the truth was to repeat what had happened when I carried Adam outside, but this time, he said, make a record of it—on 8mm film, if Agnes, a seasoned moviemaker, wouldn't mind operating the camera. Agnes agreed. As a precaution, Dr. Cohen said he would return an hour later and bring with him a small tank of oxygen and a set of instruments to perform an emergency tracheotomy if he had to, although he promised it would never come to that. Agnes suddenly looked very nervous and said she wasn't so sure this was a good idea. But Dr. Cohen assured her that her son's life wouldn't be in jeopardy, that we would rescue him before anything terrible happened.

8

THE FILM BEGINS WITH A JITTERY BLUR, THE result of the camera slipping out of Agnes's hand. So steady in her filmed chronicles of birthdays and Christmases, Agnes was too nervous and upset to do the job and handed the Bell & Howell (and the attached bar of blinding lights) over to Dr. Cohen. Before he got his bearings, the doctor managed a bumpy pan across the kitchen before settling on Adam, thin and moonfaced, dressed in khaki pants and a blue-checkered shirt. Pale and bleached out, partly because of the powerful lights, partly, I think, because he was so frightened, Adam held my one hand with both of his while I, keeping the door open with my free hand, glanced helplessly at the camera. Agnes stood behind me to Dr. Cohen's right; all a viewer could see of her was part of her floral print dress. Her tears, which Adam, Dr. Cohen, and I clearly remembered, went unseen by posterity and medical science.

In the film I brace myself, take Adam by the pants, and hoist him into the air and over the threshold, holding him suspended between indoors and outdoors. Almost immediately Adam gasps for air and his eyes roll back into his head. Dr. Cohen, seeing that Adam might be in danger, places the camera on the floor and takes Adam from me. He eases the boy to the floor, a few inches from the camera lens. Adam is screaming, his eyes twitch and bulge, his head vibrates like a machine, his nose pumps out a thin stream of brilliant red blood: all in extreme close-up.

Then you see a small explosion of orange light.

And then nothing.

The film, standard 8mm, came in fifty-foot spools, but since the roll was divided down the middle, after the first twenty-five feet, the operator was required to (in dim light or total darkness) remove the spool, reverse it, and replace it in the camera, a complicated procedure even under normal circumstances. Agnes was in no condition to try. She had had enough of making movies. Dr. Cohen took with him a roll with less than two minutes of footage, but what he had captured, he said, was more than enough.

Over the years, Adam watched the film (eventually a tape and then a DVD) again and again. He knew every frame and every detail: the frayed collar of his blue-checkered shirt; the looseness of the doorknob (so unlike me, he joked, to allow a malfunction in the house); the red-smeared plate at the edge of the frame (Dr. Cohen had eaten a piece of cherry pie minutes before the filming took place); the shadow of the flypaper that hung in the pantry; the movie lights reflected in the cabinet windows like four dazzling suns; the Latin-faced clock, reading a quarter after eleven; my windbreaker, with my Aircraft ID badge pinned to its pocket, hanging over a kitchen chair; the gray light of the chilly March day; the clouds of breath escaping from my mouth and then from Adam's; the shuddering flowers of Agnes's skirt, one blossom stained long before with a dot of tomato sauce or pie filling; Dr. Cohen's black bag and the shadow of the oxygen tank he had brought with him; the trout-like speckles of the kitchen linoleum floor.

But the image that lingered so long in Adam's thoughts and lingers in mine even now is a boy's eternally silent scream.

9

AS IT TURNED OUT, ADAM WAS OVERJOYED BY what had transpired in our kitchen. He had at last merged with his beloved house, although he couldn't say why the union had been so traumatic and painful, guessing only that the violence of it somehow ensured the permanence of it. Dr. Cohen and a few of his colleagues came over to observe young Adam, and he answered all their questions as truthfully and completely as he could. They asked Adam to talk about the house, how he and it communicated, how he and it demonstrated friendship toward each other and why, in his opinion, the house wanted him to stay within its walls, its dominion. They asked him about his dreams in which he was the *House-Adam* and destroyed other houses and crushed the children who inhabited them. The doctors were impressed by Adam's maturity, his eagerness to please, his pleasant behavior and good manners. Still, most of them wanted to place Adam under observation, as they called it, which to Agnes and me meant putting him in a hospital or asylum or some such place. Agnes and I, of course, wouldn't hear of it. Take our child from us? That was never going to happen, not in a million years.

There was one doctor, Dr. Treelore, who seemed to understand Adam's need to stay at home and our need, as parents, to keep him out of their hospitals. He sent a letter to Agnes and me:

> Adam has a cheerful buoyant intelligence, a fruitful imagination and highly developed social skills; yet he refuses (or his body won't allow him) to leave your house, making him an introvert of the first order. As far as I can tell, his identification with the house was not triggered by a single traumatic event, although such a possibility, unknown to us, can't be ruled out. At first I thought I could coax Adam out of his isolation and appeal to his rational side, but that didn't work. He was too smart for

me and could see right through me. What's more, I think his reaction to the outside world is becoming more and more negative. I can see it even in the few times I've observed him. His case is a kind of paradox. On the one hand, something's very wrong, but on the other hand, nothing's wrong at all. Right now, all I can say is just watch and wait and live your lives. Be patient, be caring, above all, be yourselves. The best path to take, I think, is to hope that the normal parts of Adam will, in time, overcome the house-animating world-wary parts. One day, Adam might need full-time medical attention, but now is not the time.

Agnes and I decided not to release Adam into the care of psychologists or psychiatrists or whatever they were, and if they tried to take Adam by legal means, we were willing to fight them to the bitter end. We even hired an attorney (a friend of my immediate superior at the Aircraft) who gave us the same advice the young understanding doctor gave us: watch and wait.

Adam's first few housebound weeks were difficult for Agnes. She had turned into a more nervous, more obsessive version of herself. She had trouble focusing, trouble making sense of anything I said to her. She didn't seem to be interested, as I was, in what caused Adam's situation. She was interested in only the consequences.

What really upset her was the possibility that Adam might spend the rest of his life in our house, a prison of his own making. Adam had given the house life, but the house hadn't given him anything and would never give him anything. It was really only a jail. It would keep him from going to high school and college, from having a career or a profession, from leading a normal productive life. And it was also possible that Adam might turn bad, become a bitter raging adult, a freakish creature who couldn't walk outside his kitchen door or stick his head out of his bedroom window. She became depressed and languished around the house convinced that her son would be a prisoner all his life and that we would be, too, forced to live in his dark, lonely half-world.

Then, a week or so later, she had a change of heart. She had made herself sick worrying about Adam, imagining dark melodramas, but she eventually understood that that kind of thinking wasn't doing anyone any good, not her, not me, and certainly not Adam.

She secretly watched him one day as he sat at his desk drawing.

She saw how consumed he was, how meticulous, moving his pencil in short, precise strokes, nothing like a child's impatient, messy spasms. Maybe, she thought, she'd been wrong. Maybe the doctors, even the kindhearted one, had been wrong, too. Maybe Adam's condition wasn't a condition at all, maybe Adam was just fine or, if not that, just a little off, a little eccentric, and maybe that was all right. Maybe she had been so busy fretting about how Adam might turn out, she had neglected to see him as he really was. The undeniable fact was that, aside from the house nonsense, Adam was a stable, even-tempered, and normal child. At an age when boys were usually spiteful and petulant, little engines of destruction, Adam was sweet natured, well mannered, and intelligent. In fact, he seemed to have an enormous heart and a profound empathy for all living things. My mother used to say he was "too good to be true" and Agnes's folks called him *chlopiec z nieba*, "a boy from heaven."

Watching Adam draw, Agnes convinced herself that she and I could, if we tried hard enough, help our son live a normal, comfortable life. Dr. Cohen and even young Dr. Treelore dropped by occasionally to check up on him, but she believed that eventually those visits would be unnecessary. The burden would be ours, Agnes's and mine, but, of course, it wouldn't be equally distributed. Since I went to work at the Aircraft every day, the responsibility of raising Adam, of teaching him, of keeping him active and curious, of downplaying his imaginary inventions, of encouraging and giving worth to what he did otherwise, would fall on Agnes's slender shoulders. But she accepted the challenge and became Adam's reluctant tutor, refusing to allow Adam to be the monster she once thought he was destined to become.

10

NEITHER AGNES NOR I KNEW IF ADAM HAD EVER been officially declared a recluse, either by Dr. Cohen or school officials or anyone else. We didn't know if such a designation actually existed. In fact, we didn't even know the word *recluse* until Agnes heard it on the television one evening.

At first Agnes and I were concerned that Adam might spend his days moping around the house, bored to tears and hopelessly despondent. Agnes dreaded, absolutely dreaded, the moment when Adam would give up any pretense of happiness and stare out the window and weep, crushed by his isolation and saddened by the fate the house had chosen for him (or he had chosen for himself). But for the first few weeks of his isolation, he appeared to be having a wonderful time. His life was not only bearable, it was thoroughly enjoyable and he seemed unwilling to give up any of it. He read books, drew pictures, devoured Agnes's dinners (especially her pies), listened to music, watched television shows and old movies and, from his bedroom window, carefully, warily observed his former classmates as they came and went from school. He didn't even mind giving up Sunday drives or visiting his grandparents in Massachusetts. In the back of our minds, Agnes and I believed the day would come when Adam would walk out the kitchen door and step out into the world again, although, being realistic or fatalistic or pessimistic or whatever you want to call it, we knew that that wasn't going to happen anytime soon.

When Adam stopped going to school, his school chums, curious about his absence, came knocking on our door asking about him. At first, Agnes was going to tell them that Adam had to stay inside for health reasons (she said something about the flu) and couldn't see visitors. But then it occurred to her that Adam might actually benefit from his school pals' visits. He might see how independent they were, free to come and go as they pleased, riding bikes and playing games and having fun, while he was stuck in his house. So rather than shoo away playmates, she asked them to drop by and keep Adam company.

That summer, the flood gates opened and the visitors arrived, some to read comics, some to play cards, some to watch cartoons on Adam's very own television (unheard of in the neighborhood), some to play Monopoly or flip baseball cards or trade PEZ dispensers. Of course, each visit was graced by generous helpings of Agnes's pie.

Agnes and I noticed that the boys (they were all boys) treated Adam as if he were sick, deferring to him, humoring him. And they were all careful about touching him or sitting too close to him. They envied Adam, at the center of a glorious universe of games and treats, but they did so from a distance, suspecting that the paradise of Adam's life was a limited one and calculating how many games and diversions would be enough to keep them happy in a world as small and narrow and confined as this.

Then something unexpected happened.

The children who visited the first few times stopped coming. Agnes wondered if Adam's "illness" kept them away, made the boys nervous, but after talking to some of their parents she learned that it was Adam who was responsible for their sudden desertion. He had asked them not to come by again, not because he had the flu or some other disease but because he didn't want to see them anymore. He was very clear and direct about it. He didn't dislike the boys and he had certainly had a lot of fun with them.

He just wanted to be by himself.

11

ADAM ONCE SAID HE HAD A BIG SECRET TO TELL me. Very early one morning, he said, when he thought Agnes and I were asleep, he walked *near* the front door and discovered that the closer he got to it the more his body was repulsed. He felt dizzy and nauseous and then he felt a tightness in his throat that made it difficult for him to breathe. When he actually touched the door or opened it, the tightness became more pronounced and his awful convulsions returned: he had to jump away from the door to stop shaking and begin breathing normally again. He did this several times, he said, until it became a kind of dance. Eventually, he got to the point where he could control the violence of his spasms and the constriction in his throat through adept footwork. That was his big secret. I said that was fine, but suggested that we collaborate on an experiment, one inspired by Adam's big secret and his former fondness for Sunday drives. Before the house had imposed itself on Adam's life, we went on a family adventure nearly every Sunday. We visited the Olszewski-Tencza farms in Massachusetts as well as public parks, war monuments, and the houses of famous men and women. We stopped at hot dog stands, clam bars, and lobster shacks. We climbed alongside gushing waterfalls and picnicked by a reservoir that collected in the hills like tea in a cup. We strolled along the shore collecting sea glass and walked hilltop trails that gave Adam a hawk's eye view of the world. None of us wanted to give up any of this, but we had no choice. Going on a Sunday drive with Adam was impossible, going without him was out of the question.

My idea was this: if Adam had become an extension of the house, then what about the garage? Wasn't that part of the house?

"It probably isn't," Agnes said, "because it's not connected to the house. Adam would have to go outside in order to get into the garage."

"Well, then," I said, "I'll connect the garage to the house."

And so I did. I built a short causeway ("the laundry room," as it would eventually be called, since it was destined to house a new Maytag washer and dryer) that linked our one-car garage to my workshop and the back side of the kitchen. My friend Witold and some of my coworkers at the Aircraft (including Otto Targonski, father to Adam's future tutor) dropped by to help and, in August 1957, the project was completed four weekends after it had begun. Now we were ready to proceed with the experiment.

It was a steamy afternoon, a hundred degrees at least. Fans whirred and rattled in every room. Adam walked between Agnes and me, holding our hands. We went the length of the connector without incident. Then I opened the door to the garage. Immediately a blast of hot air, carrying the odors of motor oil, gasoline, car exhaust, hot rubber, and dead mice struck our faces, but there we were, standing in the garage, with Adam between us, breathing normally.

"In the next part of the experiment," I announced, "things really get interesting. If our friend Adam can accept the garage as part of the house, then maybe he can also accept the car as part of the garage."

Agnes got into the passenger's seat and Adam, recalling the joy of Sunday drives past, flung himself into the back and began to giggle. I lifted the garage door. The afternoon light was blinding, like a million of Agnes's movie lights. I returned to the car, got in, and turned on the ignition. I backed out of the garage an inch at a time and went even more slowly when I reached the edge of the driveway. But we got no farther than the sidewalk on Peru Street when Adam's throat began to swell and a drop of blood, dazzlingly red in the sunlight, fell out of his nose and landed as a red asterisk on his shorts.

I drove the car back into the garage and carried Adam back into the kitchen where, a minute or two later, he became himself again. Agnes was shaking, upset that Adam had to go through yet another torture. But Adam wasn't the least bit crestfallen. In fact, he was his usual cheerful self and, showing his gratitude for my efforts and, I suppose, for adding to the house's footprint by building the causeway, he gave me a hug.

12

NOW AND THEN AGNES AND I WENT OUT TO dinner or to a party or a movie, not to get away from Adam or anything like that, but simply to have a good time. Adam didn't mind our going in the least, particularly since we hired young Angela Wrobel as babysitter.

Angela lived with her mother across the walkway, a narrow strip of property that connected Peru Street with the Kosciusko Veterans' Club on Jefferson Avenue. She was an unusually beautiful girl, a freshman in high school, with silky blond hair, sexy lips, and stunning turquoise eyes. Her movie-star looks came as no surprise to people in the neighborhood since her mother, a widow since Angela was a baby, was a big movie fan, and read those fan magazines my friend Witold sold at his variety store. Everyone on our street expected Angela to go to California one day and maybe become a movie star. A few days after she graduated from high school, she lived up to everyone's expectations: she left for Los Angeles with a young man named Chi Chi.

Adam had quite a crush on Angela and when she came over he didn't know what to do with himself. He drew pictures for her and of her, drew crazy maps for her and who knows what else. But Angela didn't babysit that often. She didn't have that many free evenings. Boys were constantly taking her to the movies or to dances or wherever. So instead of Angela coming over to sit with Adam, Mrs. Wrobel did. We thought Adam would be disappointed, considering how infatuated he was with the gorgeous Angela, but he never was. Adam enjoyed Mrs. Wrobel's company, impressed by how much she knew about movies and movie stars. They never played cards or games when she came over; they just watched movies: the *Million Dollar Movie* on Channel 9 or *Movie 4* or, if she stayed late enough, *The Late Show* on Channel 2. By her own count she had seen over a thousand movies, and not on TV or in dingy local cinemas, but in the grand theaters of New York: the Strand and the Roxy, even Radio City Music Hall. And when Mrs.

Wrobel babysat, Adam was always the perfect little host, cutting her a slice of Agnes's pie or pouring her a glass of tonic water which she drank to relieve the pain and numbness in her legs.

13

THAT HALLOWEEN, AGNES, ADAM, AND I DRESSED as hobos and had a party of our own in Adam's room. The day before I'd bought Adam a new green wingback chair and a cherry end table, which I placed directly in front of the window overlooking the walkway between our house and Mrs. Wrobel's. It would become his catbird seat, the spot from which he watched the world go by. Agnes brought in a bowl of Adam's favorite candies and later surprised him with a smaller bowl of PEZ candies, adding three new dispensers for his growing collection. We gathered by the window and waited for the afternoon light to fade. I left the party early to man my post at the front door, handing out miniature Mounds to trick-or-treaters, while Agnes and Adam tried out the new chair (he sat on her lap) and watched the children parade along the walkway on their way to and from Peru Street. They were dressed as vampires, Frankenstein monsters (with green faces and their fathers' old suit coats worn backwards), clowns, hobos like us, princesses, and ballerinas. A few children dressed as robots or Martians or Sputnik babies or children of the future. Soon, Adam began to notice that the children, and more than a few accompanying parents, glanced up at his window as they walked by, some uneasily. Agnes noticed it, too. Later, in bed with me, she wondered if the neighborhood's perception of Adam had changed, from gentle little boy to dark unsettling presence. Recluse Adam had always been a curiosity to the neighborhood kids, but maybe he'd become something freakish and threatening.

As I handed out candy downstairs, I noticed that nearly all of the children, once they had accepted my mini-Mounds, deposited candy of their own at the side of the front door. Soon a large pile accumulated. The candies left were generally the least-liked varieties but, even so, Agnes and I were astonished by the sheer quantity of the treats. Agnes thought it was a form of tribute: the kids were buying off Adam so he wouldn't haunt them or invade their dreams or do something just as creepy. I thought it was a collective act of kindness and neighborliness (I was careful not to use the word pity).

Over the years, leaving candy at 7 Peru Street became a custom in our neighborhood. Every Halloween, children, for reasons they probably couldn't explain, left Adam their second-class candies and gums, the oranges and apples given to them by old ladies, the bags of crumbling pretzels, the dry cupcakes wrapped in weepy plastic, and the little pouches of clumped-together candy corn. And it didn't stop when Adam reached adulthood, except for those years when children stopped going out for Halloween, fearing people who hid razors in caramels and coated M&M's with poison, monsters much more fearsome than the recluse Adam Olszewski.

14

A WEEK OR SO BEFORE ADAM'S NINTH BIRTHDAY, a nor'easter dropped two feet of snow on our city. That night, as the snow began to taper off, we were in the den watching television when we heard a resounding thump. I thought it might be masses of snow dropping off the roof, but then another thump followed, accompanied by the angry roar of an engine. I ran to the front door and saw that one of the city's plows had piled a mountain of snow against the corner of the house and was now ramming into it again and again. From where I stood, it appeared that the driver of the plow was trying to push the snow forward without realizing there was a house behind the pile.

I rushed outside, waving my hands above my head, signaling the driver to stop, which he did, but only after slamming the plow into the mountain one last time. I pulled the driver out of the cab and began screaming into his face. Then I came inside to call the police.

"The man's drunk," I told Agnes. "He can barely stand up."

When the police arrived, the driver had abandoned his plow and made his way through the snow down Mexico Street (an hour or so later he gave himself up at the police station downtown). At eleven o'clock, workers from the public works department arrived: a plow driver and three young men with shovels who leveled the mountain and cleared the street in short order. Meanwhile, I went to the parlor to see if the wall had been breached. It had. There was a serious crack in the plaster that extended from just below the ceiling to just above the floor. When I went to my workshop for some tape and plastic sheets, Adam went over to feel the cold air seeping through the fissure. He became dizzy and a little shaky and had to sit on the sofa to keep from fainting. The outside world had ever so slightly penetrated into the house and was affecting Adam just as it had in the kitchen the year before, nearly to the day.

In the early morning, Adam said he heard the house wheeze and cough, its normal breathing disrupted by the gash in its front wall; and now and then, he added, it seemed to sigh deeply, as if impatient for the wound to heal and the pain to go away. At breakfast, Adam asked me if he could see the damage the drunken driver had inflicted on the outside of the house. I said sure and told him to look out the front window. Then I found an old mirror I'd been keeping in my workshop and carried it into the middle of Peru Street. I held the glass in front of my face, maneuvering it this way and that so finally Adam could see the wound for himself, a wide, black toothless smile across the side of the house.

"It's quite a gash," I called out, "but it could have been worse."

The next few days were mild and sunny and soon the snow was mostly gone. A group of workers came over to repair the plow's damage, at the city's cost; and the house, rebuilt and repainted inside and out, passed the night, according to Adam, in comfort.

15

AFTER HIS NINTH BIRTHDAY, ADAM NOT ONLY refused to leave the house, he refused to leave even his room. Agnes and I saw it coming. We sensed a profound change taking place in his personality (he became more sullen and more despondent) and in his relationship with the house. Agnes spoke with him about it and he confessed that whatever was bad about the outside (he refused to or could not elaborate) had infiltrated and compromised the inside. It had crept into the kitchen and den and living room—just like the cold air that seeped into the house after the drunken plowman had done his worst. For Adam, the house was no longer secure, no longer a fortress, and it could no longer protect him. Adam didn't blame the house. It was just that the bad parts of the outside world had become much more powerful.

So on that day in spring he simply locked the door and stayed in his room. When he didn't come down for breakfast, we called up to him. Finally, when we knocked on his bedroom door, he begged us to understand and, after hours of arguing and cajoling, we agreed to let him have his way. We had to. He was hysterical at this point. We called Dr. Cohen and the young doctor who had been so kind to Adam in the past and they said to give in to the boy: it was simply too risky to bring him anywhere for evaluation. The kind young doctor said this was abnormal behavior and might indicate something more serious, some kind of mental disorder. He said it was possible that Adam might harm himself (become suicidal) and/or others (meaning Agnes and me). But he soon amended his assessment and said it was *possible* that these bad things could happen, but not *likely*. Agnes, however, didn't hear or didn't want to hear the doctor's caveat and sunk into a depression that lasted for days.

Adam not only refused to leave his room, he refused to see anyone: not us, not his grandparents, not even the resplendent Angela or his beloved Mrs. Wrobel. He even refused to allow Dr. Cohen to examine him. What's more, we no longer ate meals as a family or watched the television or did anything together. When Agnes or I brought food to him, we knocked our special knock (mimicking the first four notes of Beethoven's Fifth), and left the food on a cheap metal table in the hallway. We then retreated as Adam opened his door and carried the table into his room. When we talked, we talked through his door. Agnes and I kept two folding chairs in the hallway. We sat on them, our knees touching, whenever we spoke with our son. That happened once an evening, usually after supper.

At first Adam was eager to talk with us through the door. To him, it meant that he and Agnes and I and the house (whose door it was, after all) were at last together. We were truly a family in his eyes. He talked mostly about childish things. About cartoons or television shows, about some new toy, about his collection of PEZ dispensers. He especially liked gossip about his neighborhood chums, particularly Jake.

Agnes and I knew how foolish we looked sitting on folding chairs in front of Adam's door, suffering through long silences as we waited for him to reply to something we said or else listen to him jabber about some silly toy or children's book. When we urged (and often begged) him to leave his room, when we told him it wasn't normal that we three should be separated like this and it wasn't right that a father and mother couldn't see their only child, he became silent. He never argued with us. He just refused to talk with us, punishing us for complaining, for disrespecting or insulting or simply not including his beloved house. Sometimes he wouldn't talk to us for days on end and never told us why. We had no choice but to play according to his rules. We were being manipulated by a nine-year-old boy. We were being bulldozed and blackmailed. How pathetic we were, I said, to allow all this to happen. But Agnes didn't agree. She did everything he wanted without complaint. Knowing that she couldn't see him, she became desperate for and would do anything to hear his voice through his bedroom door.

In time, Adam created his own world in that bedroom of his. He had his own television and his own radio. Later, I bought a shortwave radio so he could listen to broadcasts from London and Paris and Eastern Europe. He also had his own record player, a children's model with the image of some cowboy or other on its case. The older he got, the more advanced and more grown up his record player (now a stereo) became. We kept him supplied with paper, paints, pencils, crayons, and plenty of books and records. He really didn't ask for that much. Just things to pass the time. He kept up with the news and was knowledgeable about current events, unusual in a child his age.

Dr. Cohen was completely stumped by Adam's behavior. He said a few of his colleagues wanted to enlist a handful of burly orderlies and storm the room, sedate Adam, and transport him to the local hospital for examination. But Dr. Cohen wouldn't hear of it. He knew better. He had seen firsthand Adam's reaction to the outside world and, of course, he had the roll of 8mm film, which he played for any psychologist or psychiatrist who was willing to sit through it. Often, he played it for himself to make sure he was doing the right thing by allowing his young patient to remain where he was. Yes, he said, Adam could be successfully sedated, but then what? He would have to wake up somewhere and that somewhere had to be outside his room and, worse, outside his house. No one knew what Adam would do in a hospital room or any other strange environment. He could be kept under sedation, but what was the good in that? Why would he and everyone else go to the trouble of bringing Adam to the hospital only to keep him in a coma? Adam was not a threat to anyone. He didn't display violent behavior and wasn't often depressed. He was, as always, a nice boy, just one who was deathly afraid of everything and everyone around him. The doctors had no cure for that. They prescribed pills that mostly made Adam groggy and uncommunicative, something Agnes, hungry for any kind of contact with her boy, couldn't abide.

16

MORNINGS, AGNES LEFT A FOOD TRAY IN FRONT of Adam's door, went downstairs for thirty minutes or so, returned, removed the tray, and then sat on her folding chair in front of Adam's door and began the day's lessons. At noon, she went downstairs, made Adam's lunch, brought it upstairs, waited thirty minutes, and then resumed her place in the hallway to continue teaching until three o'clock. One time, however, after Agnes brought Adam his lunch, she hid on the stairwell, hoping to get a glimpse of her son as he stepped into the hallway to pick up the tray. A few minutes later, Adam opened the door, but he didn't step into the hallway. Instead, he reached out his arms, grabbed the tray by the corners, and dragged it into his room. Agnes played this trick a number of times, hoping Adam would forget and step out of his room to pick up his tray, but it never happened. If he actually spotted Agnes hiding at the top of the stairs he never let on. I think he just assumed she was there and acted accordingly.

Agnes told me that she often had the urge to bust into Adam's room when he opened the door to get his food. She imagined the scene countless times, she said, taking him by surprise, rushing into the room, grabbing him around the waist, forcing him to look at her. But she couldn't do it. She just didn't know what would happen to him. Would he faint, bleed from the nose, choke on his own spit? She had no idea.

To be honest, I thought Agnes would eventually torment herself to the point of nervous collapse. To be a mother and yet never see, never touch her child was an impossible situation. We often told Adam so in the little talks we had together. We said we loved him and we wanted to look at his face and hold him in our arms. We promised not to harm him, we promised to obey the house's commands, we promised to make him happy. But Adam never replied.

Through it all Agnes held her ground. She didn't collapse when she had every reason to. She didn't withdraw into herself, didn't stare out windows with eyes glazed over, didn't see a doctor, didn't lose sleep, or have a single nightmare. Agnes dearly loved her child, but there was something in her constitution, a blind stubbornness and competitiveness, that refused to let this (or any) situation get the best of her. And her refusal to surrender was so focused, so narrow in its band, that it didn't spill over into the rest of her life, didn't contaminate her relationships with me or anyone else. It was as if she had performed a kind of psychological surgery on herself.

17

A NUMBER OF ADULT VISITORS KNOCKED ON OUR door during the first year of Adam's reclusion. One was Mr. Gazza, who said he was associated with the city's Board of Education, although Agnes suspected he was really a truant officer of some kind. He might have known something about Adam's situation from the board's records or from neighborhood gossip, but he never got to speak with Adam. Agnes wouldn't allow it, of course. He came over a number of times ostensibly to talk about Adam's education. He always dropped by in the afternoon when I was at work, which I didn't like one bit. At first Mr. Gazza was curious why Adam was no longer a student at St. Paul's and nodded sympathetically when Agnes told him that her son suffered from a psychological disorder and asked him to call Dr. Cohen for details. The next time he visited, this time with a policeman (a large, bulky man nearing retirement who didn't speak a word the whole time he was in our house), he asked the same question and Agnes politely gave him the same answer; and when, on another visit, he asked the question a third time, she became angry and asked Mr. Gazza why he had deliberately ignored what she had previously said and why he had never called Dr. Cohen for verification. Mr. Gazza apologized profusely and went on to talk more abstractly about the school versus the home as the proper seat of education.

All along I suspected that Mr. Gazza was visiting our house for reasons that had nothing to do with Adam's education. Agnes, after all, was a very attractive woman. It was clear to me that the creepy little man (Agnes's description) was out to steal her heart. When he came to visit, he was always dressed in a suit and had splashed enough cologne on himself that even Adam, upstairs in his room, could pinpoint the exact instant of his arrival. He usually brought gifts, although nothing so obvious as flowers or candy. Once, he brought a book on the socializing function of formal education, once an Easter butter lamb from St. Paul's, and once a Hardy Boys mystery for Adam (which Adam refused to look at). Eventually, Mr. Gazza's semiamorous snooping and just-in-the-neighborhood visits became unbearable. Agnes called Dr. Cohen and explained the situation. She later learned that the good doctor, always Adam's champion (and now hers), talked to a few board members, telling them that Mr. Gazza ought to find something better to do with his time. The little man never came by again.

18

AGNES WAS ADAM'S TUTOR DURING THOSE EARLY years, but she doubted she was or would ever be a proper teacher for her son. She had left school at an early age. She had difficulty writing and her reading skills were no match for Adam's. But she forged ahead. She enlisted my help to plan a curriculum and create lesson plans, mostly in reading, vocabulary, and spelling. She was fairly comfortable with arithmetic, since at one time she had helped manage the books for our parents' business and had once thought about a career as a bookkeeper. All in all, she managed to stay one day ahead of Adam, studying late into the night to do so. She progressed page by page by page, never skipping chapters, never jumping ahead.

Agnes did remarkably well considering she spent every one of her teaching hours talking to Adam's bedroom door. She expected him to read out loud, answer questions, pay attention and do homework, all of which he did conscientiously (he left his homework outside his door every evening). Adam was an intelligent boy who had no trouble understanding the lessons Agnes tried to teach him. When the school day ended at three o'clock, he was on his own until after dinner when Agnes and I made our evening visit.

What did he do in his room? We thought he spent most of his time reading (after doing his homework, of course). He seemed to devour every book he could get his hands on. He didn't care about the subject matter; he just had to be reading *something*. I brought him piles of books from the city library on Jefferson Street: westerns, biographies, novels, books about science. Sometimes Mrs. Greco, the librarian, suggested a title Adam might like, but mostly I chose books at random. As a treat, I bought paperbacks for him at Witold's variety store by the railroad tracks downtown.

Adam also drew pictures (he was always running out of paper, it seemed) and listened to the radio and, in the evening, watched TV. Agnes could hear the muffled canned laughter of comedies coming from his room as she sat at the kitchen table, planning out the next day's lessons.

19

THAT FIRST YEAR WENT BY SLOWLY. WE WERE just learning the rules of our new situation, our new life. Then five years passed and we barely noticed their passing. Soon Adam was fourteen. The three of us had settled into a routine that was uncompromisingly, mindlessly regular. Weekdays, I went off to the Aircraft, Agnes went over the day's lessons sitting in front of Adam's door (with Adam correctly answering her every question and getting an A on every project and every exam) and, after dinner, Agnes and I spent our time with our son outside his door chatting about the news, television shows, or anything unusual that Adam had seen outside his window. Our way of life didn't seem odd to us or eccentric: it was what we had to do to keep our son at home and our little family together. Dr. Cohen came over every now and then, but only when Agnes and I were sick with a cold or a touch of flu. Adam was never ill, never needed medical attention. Dr. Cohen wasn't surprised. Adam lived in a relatively germ-free environment.

During those years, a quiet settled on 7 Peru Street. It was the quiet of routine, but it was also the quiet of learning. Agnes made dinner each night, sometimes including a pie for Adam and me. When Adam was a toddler (that is, when he was a normal little boy), Agnes was known in the neighborhood for her pies. When someone was sick, or was in mourning, or had suffered some kind of trial or catastrophe, Agnes would, without fail, stop by with one of her pies. Her visits usually lasted fifteen minutes or so, long enough for a cup of coffee or a shot of blackberry brandy, although sometimes the struggling or grief-stricken neighbor would go on and on, finding solace in the simple act of talking. The pies were never eaten during those visits. Agnes presented them only as she was leaving.

But once Adam began his hermit life, Agnes had little time for baking pies. She no longer visited her neighbors, no longer tried to provide ease and comfort for those who had been in the hospital, or had suffered some grave financial setback, or whose son or daughter had been in a car accident. When Adam became a recluse, Agnes and I became hermits of a sort ourselves. Mrs. Wrobel continued to be our babysitter and she and Adam would watch movies on the television together: Adam on the set inside his room and Mrs. Wrobel on a portable placed in the hallway on a fold-up chair. When Adam got older, she would come over just to visit. They'd either watch movies on their pair of televisions or else she'd regale him with stories of grand theaters and movie star bios. Occasionally she'd have dinner with Agnes and me and tell us what was going on in the neighborhood: who had left, who had married, who had died. Other people, such as my friends from the Aircraft and Agnes's friends from our pre-Adam days, met us at restaurants or clubs, never at our home.

We learned from Mrs. Wrobel that people in the neighborhood (especially the children and old people) thought of us as ghosts: no longer there, even though they could see me coming home from work at night and see Agnes tending her garden or sunbathing on her chaise lounge during her and Adam's lunch hour. Our home, she reported, was a kind of haunted house to them, a place of mystery and strangeness.

20

ONE DAY AFTER LUNCH, AGNES WENT UPSTAIRS to resume her tutoring and discovered that Adam had left several large piles of papers outside his door. She quickly realized the piles contained Adam's drawings: all the way back to his toddler days. He hadn't thrown anything away, not a sketch, not a doodle; in addition there were scraps with poems and little stories on them. Everything he had put to paper he had saved and, on top of it all, was a single note asking us to archive his work (chronologically: everything was dated), preferably in a metal cabinet that could withstand fire and natural disasters. When Agnes asked him why he had saved everything and why he was so protective about his poems and sketches, he simply said: "How else would anyone know me?"

That evening, Agnes and I went through his drawings. They went from his first, unsure, childish attempts to accomplished watercolors, ink drawings, and pencil sketches of shoes, or a chair, or a door knob, or anything else he found in his room. What struck me immediately about the drawings was their repetition. There wasn't one sketch or painting of his toothbrush, there were dozens of them, usually from different angles or in different media. It was a sad commentary on our boy's creative life: if he was putting a mirror to his world, it was a small mirror and a sadly small world.

He was also interested in drawing maps. At one point he asked us for atlases, historical and otherwise, and road maps, which he then copied with painstaking accuracy. Later, after his tutor was on the job, his maps became more inventive and whimsical, even silly.

Agnes was up past midnight searching through all the piles, studying each drawing, each painting, each map.

"I was hoping to find something," she said when she finally came to bed. "But it wasn't there."

"What? What were you looking for?"

"A self-portrait."

21

AGNES AND I ALWAYS THOUGHT THAT ONE DAY Adam would simply walk out of his room and out of the house and into the world again, a resurrected young man. But that never happened. When Adam was still fourteen, we no longer knew if the house had any hold on him at all, if his confinement was the result of powerful house-generated forces, or Adam's own will, or simple routine. We had asked him that very question time and time again: why did he remain a prisoner in his room? We never expected an answer and never got one. But one evening was different.

"The house," he said through the door, "is still me and I'm still it. If you want men from the mental hospital to bust down the doors and take me away, go right ahead, but a minute or two after I leave this room I'll be dead."

A cleverer couple might have found a way to trick Adam into leaving his room, but not us. Everything we did concerning Adam we did for two reasons: to keep Adam happy and content and to keep him out of a mental hospital. So, you see, the three of us were both working toward the same goal. Adam, Agnes, and I wanted Adam home and happy. Of course, we hated that we couldn't see our son, couldn't touch him, couldn't embrace him, but maybe, we thought, that was the price we had to pay to keep him.

22

DID ADAM MISS ANY PART OF THE LIFE HE LIVED before he became a recluse? Did he miss riding his bike or playing with his mates in the playground or taking walks or exploring the stores downtown? Not that we could tell. What's more, I don't think he even missed visiting his grandparents, which was too bad. As a boy, Adam had a wonderful relationship with both pairs of grandparents and loved them dearly. When we took our Sunday drives it was usually to Massachusetts to visit the family farms, staying one visit at Agnes's parents, the next one at mine. How Adam looked forward to those trips. How he loved to pick raspberries and apples and make cider, collect eggs and help with the cows. There was a point when he wanted to stay there forever and howled like a little dog when it was time to go home.

When our folks visited us at 7 Peru Street, it was usually all four of them at once (they liked doing things together, I guess), but after 1957 when Adam refused to leave the house they visited us less and less frequently. They didn't understand what was going on. We tried to explain, we even showed them the 8mm film fragment (which sent my mother running out of the room), but they still couldn't grasp why a little boy didn't want to go outside and play. They ate with him, chatted with him, played cards with him, but it wasn't enough. It was all indoors. They couldn't walk outdoors with him hand in hand and they thought there was something very wrong with that.

When Adam announced he intended to remain in his room, his grandparents were stunned. Their concern turned into a kind of grief. They found it very difficult to talk to their grandson through his bedroom door. At first it was embarrassing for them and my father wasn't afraid to tell his young namesake that he was making his parents and grandparents act like fools. But then the embarrassment turned into horror. They'd freeze in front of the door, absolutely paralyzed by the scene of adults crowding into a dimly lighted hallway and talking to a nine-year-old boy through a slab of wood. It was gravely and morbidly unnatural. They still came upstairs with us, but they didn't like it, and usually they didn't have much to say. What they did say was in quavering, timorous voices. Christmas and Easter were particularly bad for them; instead of celebrating the holidays with Adam in the hallway they remained at the top of the stairs crying into their handkerchiefs.

Nonetheless, I'm convinced Adam loved his grandparents and missed them and, even after he had sequestered himself in his room, he sometimes talked about them and the farms with a sighing, wistful nostalgia.

In 1962, Adam's grandparents began drifting away, a kind of procession of death. First my dad went (one stroke, then another, then a third and final one), then Agnes's dad (virulent lung cancer), then Agnes's mom (out of grief, I think), and my mom (undeniably out of a raw, compounded grief). In two years' time, Agnes and I were parentless and Adam had no relatives other than us. We tried to sell the farms, but without success. The real estate agent said we were asking too high a price, but Agnes insisted that it was more than property we were selling: it was a business and a fairly successful one at that and one with plenty of room for expansion. Finally, Agnes relented and we lowered the price considerably. It was too much to operate the farms long distance, and we couldn't find anyone we trusted to manage the apple-picking and cider business in the fall. Three years after my mom died we sold the farms and business to a young couple from Boston who had made their money as stock brokers and were looking to escape what they affectionately called the rat race. In June 1965, Agnes and I met them at my parents' home (they had plans to turn the house where Agnes grew up into a kind of general store) and we signed the papers. It seemed to me that Agnes and I were like generals signing a surrender.

23

One morning Agnes said she was sick of teaching (and "talking to a door") and asked that I stay home from the Aircraft for the day and give her a break. I agreed, of course, and, for the first time in my life, I called in sick. My manager at the plant was so astonished that he called back to make sure everything was all right. I didn't vary from Agnes's lesson plan and spent the morning teaching lessons in math, English, and geography. After lunch, I told Adam he could have the rest of the day off (an announcement greeted with utter silence). I left my seat in the hallway and went off to find Agnes. I peered out from an upstairs window and found her sunbathing in her black one-piece swimsuit. She had wheeled out her creaky wooden chaise-lounge to a spot between the tomatoes and gladioli where it was sunniest. It was late August and many of Agnes's tomatoes had already been eaten or given away to neighbors. The gladioli were so brightly colored they looked like elaborate confections made from spun sugar. Because it had been a hot, rainless summer, many of her plants had already sunk into the earth or had begun adopting the muted darker colors of the coming season. The lilies of the valley were already striped yellow and brown, the day lily leaves were spotted, shrunken, and crabbed.

I watched in silence as Agnes rubbed a mixture of iodine and baby oil (her own concoction) on her legs. I smiled. If anyone deserved a day off it was she. She worked so hard at being Adam's mother and teacher, but no matter how thorough she was in preparing her lessons or how enthusiastic she was in teaching them, she sensed that her son was becoming less and less interested in what she had to say. I noticed it too, indirectly, in how languid he seemed, how flagging his responses were. I also noticed how tired Agnes looked. She was always sighing, it seemed: deep, dispirited sighs.

She looked up from her magazine and saw that I was watching her from the upstairs window. She smiled, waved, threw me a kiss.

How dark she was, I thought, like a shadow, and how pale I was by comparison, like a glowworm. That evening, Agnes said she had become very aware of her limitations as a teacher. Adam was bored, frankly, and losing interest in the learning process. She said her tenure as Adam's teacher shouldn't last much longer. Adam was too smart for her. He would soon need a more advanced teacher, someone, as she said, with "a proper education."

MRS. B.

IN AUGUST 1964, A FRIEND OF MINE FROM Silverton, a dumpy little factory town not far from the dumpy little city of Hartford, told me she had heard of a local woman eager to hire a tutor for her reclusive fourteen-year-old boy. The woman, Agnes Osomething, had been serving as the boy's tutor but had apparently done all she could in that regard. There was nothing more she could teach her son. He was light years ahead of her in every subject.

I was, at the time, very much a forlorn and unsettled woman. My daughter, who had grown up in fancy suburbs and comfortable university towns, had changed, a few summers before, from a thoughtful and affectionate child to an insolent, cheerless junkie and died from a heroin overdose. A month after that, my husband, the ineluctable Fish, left me and, at the time I interviewed for the tutoring position, was still nowhere to be found. My life, it seemed to me back then, had been marred by two sorrows, one, a tragic death, and the other, a tragedy lacking the denouement of death.

I had been an adjunct professor at a number of colleges and had some success as a poet, although there was a time when I told a therapist that I had grown to despise literature almost as much as I had grown to despise young people. During most of 1962 and early 1963, I had been a patient in a private (and in literary circles highly regarded) mental hospital. My parents, crushed by the sadness that had crushed me, paid for my stay and therapy. I had little to say to my doctors, nurses, and fellow patients. I was too stunned, too hurt to speak, unable even to form the words in my mouth. What ultimately helped me had nothing to do with my medications or with electroshock therapy (the vile surge of power through the seat of my powerlessness); it was my discovery that, even in my collapse, I was just another woman trying to make something of my life.

I was released into my parents' care but I soon realized I had to earn a living. Teaching at a college was out of the question. Too much anxiety. I did some substitute work at a local high school, but even that was stressful; the students, who had somehow heard of my travails and predicament, were vicious and heartless. That was when my friend told me about Mrs. Osomething and, well, being a tutor seemed like the ideal way to earn money and not overexert myself. Teaching one boy was much easier than teaching dozens of spoiled, whiney brats. And it paid better!

During my interview, I got the sense that Mrs. Osomething had her doubts about me. We met in her strange gray house that seemed very dark to me and very, very clean. A house haunted by obsessively neat spirits. Mrs. Osomething was rather dark herself. I thought she might be a gypsy. She looked at me as if I weren't quite all there and, of course, she was right. I wasn't. I was a ghost somehow amalgamated with living flesh and blood. I think Mrs. Osomething took pity on me a little, but she hired me not because of her compassionate nature but because of my credentials. I had gone to and taught at the best schools. I didn't know anything about Mrs. Osomething, but I sensed that she was a sharp woman, not at all flighty or frivolous. She seemed to be a natural businesswoman, someone who knew the score, knew about the exigencies of life, knew how to handle herself.

I assumed she had gone to college, but when I made a common literary allusion it went right over her head. Finally, I asked her point blank where she had gone to school.

"I didn't," she said and refused to elaborate. I found her to be just as guarded about her son. She offered no explanation as to why he was a recluse, except that he had some kind of psychological condition. I was suspicious about all this, but despite my reservations, I agreed to be Adam's tutor. And oh yes, there was one more thing Mrs. Osomething didn't mention: her brilliant son never left his room and never allowed human eyes to gaze upon him. In short, I would be teaching a goddamn door! Isn't there a poem by Catullus in which the door tells the poet of all the unspeakable things someone is doing to his dear lovely Lesbia?

It was the lowest point of my life—when I had to agree to something incredible and absurd and without dignity because *I needed the money*. God, how I hate those words.

But I gave it the old college try. I did my best to be engaging, friendly, easy going, thoughtful, informative, interesting, but I simply couldn't overcome the cold and maybe even hostile—who knew for sure?—silence behind the door. Oh yes, I could definitely sense—based on the depth and number of sighs, throat-clearings, and deep breaths—that Adam didn't like me the least bit. Perhaps it was because I still wasn't quite myself, someone disconnected and vague, a woman only half there. Perhaps it was because young Adam and I were so much alike, both believing the world terrified and disappointed.

And, really, Mrs. Osomething hadn't been honest about Adam and she certainly hadn't helped me prepare me for him. She told me that the eternally unseen Adam wasn't sullen, but he was sullen. She said he wasn't caustic and cynical, but he was caustic and cynical. She said he wasn't cold and aloof, but he was cold and aloof. And, of course, Mrs. Osomething (a former chambermaid at the Hotel Silverfish, by the way) had preceded me in the position, which meant that I couldn't win. I couldn't possibly compete with dearest mumsy.

As I was leaving that dismal house, Mrs. Osomething handed me a check, payment for two days' work. She said she didn't believe anyone should work for nothing. I replied that the check wasn't necessary, that I really hadn't earned the money. I thought that Mrs. Osomething would put up a fight—had she no sense of social etiquette?—and insist more rigorously that I take the check, but she didn't. Instead, she tore it up right in front of my eyes.

"Suit yourself," she said.

At that point, Mrs. Osomething looked at me as if I had committed some kind of crime. It was clear she had no respect for me. I was despicable to her. I had no inner strength, no toughness of spirit, no fight, no gumption. And I didn't care a damn for her brat. It was amazing that in so short an amount of time, a matter of a few days, I had grown to dislike Mrs. Osomething more than I disliked anyone in my life. And the feeling, I sensed, was mutual.

MISS T.

1

MY NAME IS BEATRICE TARGONSKI, BUT SINCE Mrs. Olszewska and Adam had called his first tutor Mrs. B. as a kind of rancorous joke—Agnes never had to explain what the *B* stood for—they decided the new tutor should be called Miss T.—a nickname I accepted and eventually came to like and, finally, cherish.

In September 1964, I was a shy, wispy young woman who had that June received my degree in elementary education (music). The trouble was I hadn't been hired by any school system in the state—it was as though I had some kind of pedagogical plague. I was also a fairly accomplished pianist and gave lessons in the evening to a handful of students and so I survived—it was how Chopin made ends meet, too. I heard about the tutoring job from my pop, Otto Targonski, a deburrer at the Aircraft and a pal of Mr. Olszewski, who was, I suppose, his boss, or one of them. Pop came home one night and said the Olszewski boy—a no-kidding, honest-to-goodness hermit—was in need of a teacher. Mr. O. told pop about the position because my pop was always bragging about me and also, I think, because Mr. O. felt sorry for him because of his wife—poor mom had been suffering for years with some kind of stomach disorder that turned out to be cancer. At that point she hadn't much longer to live. In fact, she died the day before I began as Adam's tutor, postponing my first day on the job by two weeks.

My interview with Mrs. Olszewska went well, at least as far as I was concerned. She was relaxed and easy going and made me feel the same way, too. She asked a few poignant questions, but they weren't—as they often are in interviews—daggers into your soul. She mostly talked about her son, what a smart kid he was and what a nice boy—respectful and polite. When Mrs. Olszewska offered me the job, I was absolutely delighted but then—in a sudden blubbery outburst—I confessed that the reason I hadn't been hired by any school was because I had performed so poorly as a student teacher. I'd been unable to control my students and keep order in the classroom. I'd been given a passing grade only because I was imaginative in my approach and could create fabulous lesson plans—a good teacher *in theory*. But as for actually teaching—actually standing up in front of a class, imparting knowledge, and maintaining order—I had failed miserably. In truth, before Mrs. Olszewska called, I had already considered taking a detour from what my guidance counselor liked to call my career path.

But for some reason, my confession only reinforced Mrs. Olszewska's high opinion of me. It showed—as she later said in a confession of her own—that I was a young woman of character, willing to tell the truth even if it meant losing a job. When Mrs. Olszewska repeated her offer, I—generally weepy anyway because of my mother's failing health—accepted again, this time boohooing with lavalike tears gushing from my eyes.

I'm *el blimpo* now, a cow out to pasture, but back then, I was a skinny malink. I had a heart-shaped face; a long neck; thin, bloodless lips; a pointy nose; short, straight black hair; large, flawless teeth; pale cheeks—where ne'er a rose dared bloom—and, behind my scholarly, black-framed glasses; thick, black eyebrows; thin, black lashes; and flat, brown eyes. My aunt—an empress of faint praise—said I was pretty *in my own way* and had the beauty of innocence—although it soon became clear to anyone who knew me that I wasn't in the least bit innocent, or demure, or dainty, either. In all honesty, most people found my thinness disturbing. I looked like a sickly emaciated little girl who'd just escaped from the camps. Mrs. Olszewska told me that when I came to 7 Peru Street for my initial interview, I looked more like a student than a teacher. Not only was I scrawny and brittle but I wore girlish clothes and spoke in a girl's thin small voice. She said it wasn't difficult to understand why I couldn't keep a roomful of schoolchildren under control. I had no presence, no authority. I mumbled. I was a spazz. Why, of course my schoolchildren took advantage of me—they didn't think of me as an adult!

Despite my failings, Mrs. Olszewska liked me. I was considerate and well-mannered and—what really mattered in her mind—I was an *A* student throughout high school and college. And once she realized that I was also a pianist, she—shrewd businesswoman even then—asked if I would include giving little concerts now and then for her and Mr. O. as part of the tutelage package. I said yes, of course, but noted she didn't have a piano. Well, one—an upright—appeared in the den the day after I started work.

The job was perfectly suited for me. It was: (1) convenient—my pop and I lived only a few blocks away on Walnut Street; (2) intellectually challenging—not only was Adam a gifted and enthusiastic student he was also invisible (how many teachers can say they teach students they never get to see?); (3) financially rewarding—the Olszewskis paid me close to what I would have earned as a first-year teacher; and (4) healthy—Mrs. Olszewska promised she would fatten me up with lunches and even dinners that would frequently conclude with her irresistible pies.

2

WHEN I WALKED THROUGH THE FRONT DOOR OF 7 Peru Street on my first day of work it seemed that the house held darkness prisoner. Daylight stayed where it was and didn't penetrate inside. On that first day, I expected the darkness to hide correspondingly dark odors—fetid and musty and unpleasant—but that wasn't the case at all. The rooms were all spotless and smelled lilac-sweet with an after scent of bleach and—near the kitchen—more often than not, the glorious perfume of baking pies. I had no problem at all adjusting to the darkness. Because of my fair skin, I'd always avoided direct sunlight as much as possible anyway. Adam and I, it seemed, were both children of the shadows.

I arrived with a backpack filled with books, holding in one hand my pop's old lunch pail containing a cucumber and mayonnaise sandwich and a dehydrated valencia orange. Under my mustard cloth coat, I wore a pink gingham dress that looked like a picnic tablecloth. It was billowy and wrinkled and fell well below my knees. I wore black flats with white ankle socks and around my wrist was a silver charm bracelet with silver g-clefs, rests, and eighth notes hanging from it—a gift from my pop. From the outset Adam seemed to like me—which was exactly what Mrs. Olszewska had hoped for and what the impressively credentialed Mrs. B. couldn't manage. For the first time in a long time, she said, Adam's voice behind the door had some life to it—it wasn't the tired voice of a sullen teenager, but the nearly breathless voice of an enthusiastic student. Maybe I could become the everyday friend Adam never had—I was, after all, only seven years his senior. She thought Adam and I were kindred spirits. We were both shy—although Adam had taken shyness to a baroque level—and we were both avid readers and music lovers. And Adam indicated that he trusted me.

The truth was—which I learned later on from Adam himself—that he couldn't wait for my daily arrival, listening impatiently for my knock at the front door. I think maybe he had a crush on me, but that was okay because I kind of had a crush on him, too, even though I had no idea what he looked like. I could tell right off that he was special, a unique case. I'd never met a boy—or man or woman—so intelligent and perceptive, and I had a feeling that as Adam's teacher I was going to learn as much as I taught—maybe more.

After a few weeks on the job, I loosened up quite a bit around Adam and his parents. They soon learned that I loved to tease and that I wasn't terribly ladylike—which shocked Mr. O. and delighted Mrs. Olszewska, whose laugh was a lovely tune that went on and on before ending in a muffled trill—a lark seemed to live in her throat.

My classroom was the second-floor hallway and soon it was filled with books, notebooks, papers, and all sorts of other things. Eventually, Mrs. Olszewska had difficulty plowing through all the debris in order to bring Adam his meals. Relieved of her educational duties, she eventually found a part-time job with her friend, Danuta, working at a dry cleaner's, but that lasted about six months or so. That's when Mrs. Olszewska stayed home and started making her pies again—and that's when I stopped being such a skinny beanpole.

When I took the job, Mrs. Olszewski warned me that it wouldn't be like any other tutoring arrangement I'd ever heard of or could imagine. First of all, I wouldn't see my pupil—only communicate with him through a door that always remained closed. Second, I would spend my working day in a dark hallway sitting on a folding chair—in time Mr. O. would get me an old wooden classroom desk, the kind I sat in when I was in high school. Was it disconcerting talking to a door? At first, yes. But there was a voice behind that door, the voice of a living, breathing young man—although sometimes it felt as though I were communicating with a spirit, fleshless and bloodless, and our classes sometimes seemed like séances. For the most part, however, Adam made it easy for me. He was the sweetest, kindest boy. He was cooperative, helpful and—most important—he took me seriously. My teaching in that dark hallway was no lark, no pathetic little parody of the education process. I worked hard preparing my lessons. I took them seriously—and Adam did, too. He completed his assignments, he asked questions—lots and lots of questions. We marched from one lesson to another and never once did he complain. Teaching conditions at 7 Peru Street were far from perfect—and yet they were as perfect as any young teacher could hope for.

3

ONCE I WAS EARNING A SALARY, I BECAME A young woman with prospects—no longer a financial burden to my pop, no longer a woman with a muddled future—and I was able to save a little bit, too. For the most part, I followed Mrs. Olszewska's teaching strategy—plowing through, page by page, one textbook after another. But Adam and I were on fast-forward and we raced through his lessons. In three months, Adam completed the entire freshman year curriculum—and when we then went on to higher-level subjects, the Olszewskis were very proud indeed.

My math and English sections were no different than those in the public schools—only more advanced and a lot more intense. But unlike those poor students, Adam and I got to go on to more interesting subjects—art, history, art history, geography, current events, science, literature, philosophy and, of course, music. I also came up with special seminars that Adam loved—seminars on a specific poem or poet, a specific artist or work of art, a specific scientific theory or some interesting bit of scientific history—sometimes a single geographical location, sometimes a famous battle, sometimes a symphony. And usually the lessons were connected. When we studied Darwin's theory of evolution, we also studied the geography and zoology and botany of the Galapagos and South America—and we read the novels and poems, heard the music, looked at the paintings, and studied the politics of the Victorian era. We also studied foreign languages. I taught Adam French—and we learned Polish together with help from Mrs. Olszewska, Danuta, and the young women who would, later on, come to the house to make pies.

Part of my job was to introduce Adam to the world he would in all likelihood never set foot in—a big fat irony and hardly a normal teaching model. Also, I had to contend with his nutty ideas about the dangers that existed outside his room. I learned not to argue with him on the subject, but I also refused to back off and give in to him. I told him flat out he was delusional and silly and he'd get quiet or shift the discussion to something else. He knew there was no point in arguing with me. He knew every person in the world sided with me—not him. None of it ever came between us, though. Adam was eccentric—not deranged. I refused to give up hope that he might one day outgrow those bizarre ideas of his, leave the house—and enter the world! If he didn't, he'd never *be* anything, never *do* anything—never be a grown man with an occupation, a career, a calling. What haunted every lesson of ours was the undeniable and unavoidable fact that he couldn't honestly and truly learn anything about the world unless he lived in it.

4

NOW AND THEN I BROUGHT UP RECLUSION AS A seminar subject, beginning with the early Christian hermits, the Desert Fathers, St. Paul of Thebes, St. Jerome—all of whom had survived in the wilderness in part because of their belief in the purity of the human heart and the primacy of love. It was a lesson that resonated with Adam. He liked it that the ancient recluses were sources of radiance and compassion and spiritual good. There was a difference, however. The Christian hermits felt dirtied by contact with human society—which wasn't the case with Adam. He wasn't disgusted by the human condition. He wasn't intolerant of human weakness or repulsed by human folly and stupidity. He was simply afraid of being outside his room, as if the air there was poisonous, as if we—the rest of the world—emanated deadly ultraviolet rays. He loved his parents, he liked me, and he couldn't get enough of Mrs. Wrobel and her movie stars, but there was something in the outside world that threatened him, promised to do him in—something so frightening, so dangerous, so terrible that he didn't even like to talk about it—and so he never brought it up and he wouldn't discuss it when I did. He said he *had to* live alone in his room. He seriously believed that the instant he left his room would start the short countdown to the end of his life.

His hero was Jeremy Bentham—the Hermit of Queen Square Place. Bentham wanted nothing less than to create a mathematics of happiness—*felicific calculus*—then redefine and rework the whole of civilization, basing it all on a single principle—*the greatest good for the greatest number of people.* The idea delighted Adam—but, he said, it didn't go far enough. It was, by definition, exclusionary. Someone's good fortune would still be accompanied—in whole or in part—by someone else's misfortune or loss. The Benthamic principle, he said, should be amended to—*the greatest good for all—always.*

Adam took to another of the hermit's ideas, the *panopticon*—a

Bentham-designed prison, semicircular in shape like a protractor—in which a single guard could oversee a large population of inmates in a single glance, and do so without being seen. I thought the design repulsive and inhumane, but Adam said I shouldn't think of it as a penal model—no one had ever built such a prison anyway—but as a model for his house and his life. The world might buzz around him, an enormous and complex hive—but he was always at its heart. He was always at the center of his own geography—the hermit of 7 Peru Street—all-seeing and unseen.

For Adam the world was what he saw through the rectangle of his bedroom window. I'm assuming this is true, of course, since I've never seen the inside of his bedroom—but I had imagined it and dreamed about it so often I felt as if I knew it as well as I knew my own room at home. I knew where his desk was, where he kept his pencils, where the bookshelf—built by Mr. O. when Adam was a boy—was and the TV and just about everything else.

Anyway, as I see it, the bottom of the window's rectangle was taken up by a view of the property-defining wire fence—in the summer overrun with cucumber vines—and a small part of Mrs. Olszewska's tomato garden. On the other side of the fence—running through the middle of the window's rectangle—was the walkway and, behind it, the pale blue cape owned by Mrs. Wrobel. She lived on the first floor while, over the years, renters occupied the second, mostly tired, unlucky, harmless old men whose wives had left them or who had never married—men who pumped gas or pushed brooms and walked down Peru Street with pints of Four Roses or Imperial in wrinkled, twisted brown bags sticking out of their pockets—men who paid the rent on time and gave the neighborhood children gifts and candies, thunderstruck by their innocence and gawking at them as if they were angels or rare flowers.

The walkway began at Peru Street with a cement stairway and a right angle of privet hedge that defined Mrs. Wrobel's modest front yard. It continued as an easement through the Glowac property and ended at the Kosciuszko Club on Jefferson Street—the city's main thoroughfare, and a few blocks east of downtown. Only twenty or so feet wide, the walkway was owned by the K-Club to provide its members easy access to St. Paul's Church since a great many of the Club's functions were Church-related—wedding and funeral receptions, breakfasts, fund-raising bazaars, and the like. The walkway also gave neighborhood drunks easy access to the K-Club bar—and it wasn't unusual on a warm, pleasant night for Adam, staring out his window, to watch the old men stagger home, singing love songs from the war or talking to invisible comrades. In the winter, after a big snowstorm, the neighborhood children would sled from Peru Street all the way to Jefferson. Sometimes the sledders went beyond the sidewalk on Jefferson and ended up in traffic, but this was only hearsay, the braggadocio of boys—I've heard them myself—returning with their sleds in tow, crowing about how fearless and reckless they had been and how close to death they had come, which neither Adam nor I believed for a second.

Through the far left of the window, Adam could see the front porch of the house owned by the Rocque's—the noisiest of neighbors—plus he could probably see the duplex at the corner of Peru and Bolivia Streets, with the St. Paul's spire behind it in the distance. He could also see the horse chestnut tree on Bolivia and most of Kozak's market—located in the downstairs half of a two-story building. Mr. and Mrs. Kozak and their daughter, Wanda, lived in the cramped quarters upstairs and for years had been planning a move to the suburbs. Visible at the far right of the rectangle were Mrs. Wrobel's backyard and a huge rhubarb patch—planted long ago by the late Mr. Wrobel—the Glowac's mighty but mutilated oak, and the crumbling stockade fence with its long gray spikes that the neighborhood children occasionally dislodged and used as spears.

5

AFTER A FEW MONTHS, MRS. OLSZEWSKA TRUSTED me enough to show me her collection of Adammemorabilia as I called it—an entire bookcase, built by Mr. O. of course—filled with large, elegant portfolios containing every drawing and note Adam had ever put to paper—and she was still adding to the collection. That's because Adam and I still made time for drawings and paintings and poems and such. I insisted on it. I wanted him to keep his creative spirit alive.

He usually drew one thing—a flower or tie clasp or wristwatch or pack of cigarettes—and drew it to death, looking at it from various points of view, emphasizing one aspect or another. He worked quickly—sometimes at a feverish pace—but he was quite exact about dimensions, down to the millimeter, and unerring when it came to perspective, although quite a few of his drawings paid no attention to perspective at all.

Mr. O. teased his wife because she bound Adam's body of work in such a fancy and professional way—actually she had it done at a stationery store downtown near Witold's variety store—as if they were some kind of presidential documents. And quite often, she went into the den—where the bookcase was located—and, instead of watching TV, she'd put a portfolio on her lap and make her way from beginning to end, silently turning one big page after another. There must have been thirty portfolios in that bookcase and they went from 1953 when Adam was three years old to the present. Mr. O. might have teased his wife about the portfolios, but I saw him on a number of occasions leafing through one of those big books before finding—and closely studying—one drawing or watercolor or another.

When I started as Adam's tutor, he was mostly interested in maps—his crazy atlases. When he was younger, I was told he used to pore over actual maps—memorizing locations and capitals, learning whatever there was to know about a given country in a given historical epoch. Then he began to draw his own. At first, he copied maps in his sketchpad—achieving amazing levels of precision and neatness. In the end, his maps looked exactly like the ones in his atlases.

Then he started drawing maps of the house—floor plans, really—the first few mathematically exact, but the rest of them absolutely whimsical.

Eventually, Adam began drawing maps of imagined places. He drew fanciful maps for the not-so-angelic Angela Wrobel, who lived next door and was his babysitter—but she left for California or somewhere in 1960 or 1961. Then he drew similar maps for Angela's mother, Mrs. Wrobel, the movie fan, that featured the places in movie titles—Casablanca or Fort Worth with Randolph Scott, or Timbuktu with Victor Mature. Many others followed, maps of the world but from the vantage point of his house—his bedroom window—the eye of the panopticon, the spot where all geography began.

One day, he started making maps for me, slipping them under the door when I was in the middle of some lesson. In these goofy maps of his, he created a powerful nation named Mistyland—or Miss-T-Land—an empire ruled by yours truly, a progressive and forward-thinking nation, of course, but an aggressive one as well that conquered and absorbed backward and oppressive states, turning them into civilized and tolerant democracies. Mistyland stretched all the way from his window to the Pacific Ocean and in that powerful empire cities, states, counties, rivers, lakes—everything!—were named after me—New Misty, Mistyopolis, Mistyana, San Mistio, Rio Misto, Teetown, etc., etc. I was not only flattered by all the Mistyland maps, I was awed by the sheer number of variations on my nickname he'd managed to generate.

East of his window—and extending all the way to the Atlantic—was a nation only a fraction as large, but just as powerful. It was called Freedonia—like in the Marx Brothers movie. Its capital, Adamville, was Adam's room. The two countries, Mistyland and Freedonia, were allies, mutual champions of liberty and inclusion. Whenever Mistyland went to war—against Amnesia and Sylvania or any other rogue state—Freedonia rallied to her aid. Eventually, Adam's atlases became "historical" in nature, filled with a succession of tyrannies that had become enlightened protectorates, ruled jointly by Freedonia and Mistyland and designated by green and pink stripes—green for Mistyland and pink for Freedonia. In time, the two countries merged into one—a single omnipotent, mauve empire. *Orbis unum*, Adam wrote at the bottom of the last of these maps. Not long afterward, he lost interest in his funny geography and, to my knowledge, never drew another map again.

6

I NEVER WORRIED ABOUT ADAM'S ACADEMIC prowess. He had an astonishing memory and passed every exam with perfect or near-perfect scores. I did worry about his physical fitness, however—cooped up in that room all day and all night—so I became his physical education instructor as well as his academic mentor. I created a regimen of isometrics and running in place. I also designed—with Mrs. Olszewska's permission—a vegetarian diet for the both of us. Adam said ok, mostly, I think, because I argued from a Benthamic point of view—that humans shouldn't eat at the expense of other creatures—nor should they exploit living creatures for clothing—i.e., the hide of some mistreated beast. From that day on, Adam never wore leather shoes again—only slippers or sneakers—or at least he said he didn't. But since he was indifferent to what he ate—and he ate so little anyway—taking the meat out of his diet didn't amount to a significant change. Mr. and Mrs. Olszewski continued to be meat-eaters—Mr. O. loved his sausage—but Adam and I went over to the vegetarian side and—as far as I know—he remained there for good.

7

I SOMETIMES GAVE RECITALS—WITH ADAM listening with his ear to the door—for the Olszewskis and their friends and neighbors, I assume, and later—when the pie business began—the workers. Mr. and Mrs. Olszewski loved nothing better than filling their house with music. Mrs. Olszewska adored her Chopin and I played the pieces she'd heard on scratchy 78s when she was a girl, a bouquet of nocturnes and waltzes, a polonaise and—always saved for last—that strange, sad, little mazurka in A minor. My favorite composer was Maurice Ravel and soon Mrs. Olszewska and Mr. O. were buying LPs of just about everything Ravel had composed, even the much-disdained *Bolero*. She particularly liked *Miroirs*, especially the "*Oiseaux tristes*" section, with its birds sorrowfully tweeting, and I played it for her at every recital. A few times I brought some musician friends over and we played chamber music for the Olszewskis. One time a violinist and cellist and I managed to scrape together a skeletal *Trout Quintet* and for our trouble we were invited for dinner—the recitals were on Sunday afternoons—and were stuffed with astonishing food—including chocolate cream pie at the end. Then they insisted on paying us. We refused of course, but they wouldn't hear of it.

"You're trained musicians," Mrs. Olszewska told us. "You should never play for nothing."

8

IN A MATTER OF MONTHS, I BECAME PART OF THE family. Instead of going home at three or four o'clock, I often stayed for dinner—invited, of course, by Mrs. Olszewska who, as I said, was a wonderful cook—and she and Mr. O. were terrific company. I tried to help out in the kitchen, cutting onions, that sort of thing—and carrying a tray of food upstairs, placing it in front of Adam's door and knocking our secret knock. When I returned to the kitchen, I clumped down the stairs as loud as I could, making sure Adam heard me and could get his dinner tray without fear of being seen. Mr. O., however, was on to me.

"Oh, you don't have to make such a ruckus," he said. "Adam could hear you even if you tiptoed. He's like a spider, you know, connected to everything. He must feel vibrations or something."

I usually went home after dessert—almost always taking home a helping of pie for pop—but a few times I stayed. I don't know why. Maybe I was just curious. On those occasions, Mr. and Mrs. took two folding chairs and carried them to the second floor and placed them in front of the door. I was asked to sit in my usual place—my school desk. Adam had finished eating by the time we came upstairs. The tray was on the floor, the plate of food only half or quarter eaten.

"Adam's not a big eater," Mr. O. said. "If it weren't Agnieszka's cooking he probably wouldn't eat anything."

When everyone had a seat, Mr. O. knocked four times on the door and then they chatted away. Nothing earth-shattering—just a review of what went on during the day. He told them about what he had learned, Mr. O. talked about the Aircraft, Mrs. Olszewska talked about someone in the neighborhood who was sick or just got married or just had a baby girl, and I just talked about whatever came into my head—music mostly. Those after-dinner talks with Adam weren't exactly easy—there were plenty of awkward silences and pauses—certainly not the steady chatter, the give and take, of our school lessons. Being there at night with Adam and his parents was stranger than being there with Adam alone. In the morning and afternoon, his voice gave answers, asked questions, went off on digressions of all kinds, at night his voice was quiet, unsure, deferential—the voice of a loving and dutiful son. At night I got the full impact of his condition, his isolation and loneliness, his parents' grief and desperate willingness to do anything to make their son happy.

It was at their nightly visits in front of Adam's door when Mr. O. and Mrs. Olszewska left him his supplies, as Mr. O. called them: books, cigarettes—yes, he was a big-time smoker, just like the heroes of his beloved movies—drawing paper, writing paper, pencils, tubes of watercolors, magazines, sweets, treats, and all sorts of other things, from soap to soda pop. Adam had his own shower as well as a little refrigerator. Mr. O. used to say that Adam had a miniature version of the house in his room. The one thing he lacked was Agnes's stove.

9

AT ONE-HOUR MARTINIZING ON WILLOW STREET, Mrs. Olszewska and Danuta and a handful of other women were relegated to the back of the store, dry-cleaning clothes or doing special tailoring and custom cleaning jobs. The shop was a terrible place to work—and probably the very worst place to be on a summer's day—but for Mrs. Olszewska it was better than just hanging around the house. Since she wasn't Adam's tutor any longer, she had plenty of free time—and this she couldn't stand. She made plenty of pies but there were only so many sick neighbors—and Mr. O. and I and Adam could eat only so much.

Mrs. Olszewska usually came home from the cleaners at one or two o'clock. Sometimes she ate lunch with Adam and me, sometimes she brought Danuta along with her, sometimes she skipped lunch altogether and went about cleaning the house or doing her errands or baking a pie, and sometimes she and I left Adam to his own devices and went shopping or just took a walk to the park—a kind of female bonding.

On a Monday afternoon—it was around four o'clock—in June 1965, she walked over to Kozak's Market for a few groceries. I went along to get a few items for my pop. Mr. Kozak, a large man with large hands and a large, lumpy nose, never engaged in gossip or small talk with his customers. He was all business, that man, and not much fun—but his meats were far superior to what you could get at any of the grocery chains, or at least Mrs. Olszewska thought so. And, she claimed, he never added the weight of his thumb to the price of his meat. Mr. Kozak and his wife—famous in the neighborhood for her love of Bloody Marys—and their logy, dull-eyed daughter, Wanda, lived in the rooms above the store, but they were getting ready to move to a new house at the edge of town. Mrs. Kozak had recently been ill with an intestinal flu—or so her hubby claimed; everyone else knew it was the vodka that did her in—and Mrs. Olszewska had brought her a pumpkin pie to help with her recuperation. When we walked into the store that afternoon, Mr. Kozak stuck his head out of the meat-cutting room in back to thank Mrs. Olszewska for the pie and to say hello to me, his favorite customer, he said, because I was "a college girl"—the unspoken comparison, of course, was to his daughter who was something of a lazy slug.

"Oh, Mrs. Olszewska, I can't say enough about that pie of yours. Baking it just for the Missus was such a nice thing for you to do, such a neighborly thing. Thank you again."

"You're very welcome," Mrs. Olszewska replied. "I hope Mrs. Kozak is feeling better."

"Oh, she is, she is. But it was terrible, that intestinal flu. The poor woman couldn't sleep, couldn't keep anything down, except your pie, thankfully. It's what saved her. It was like medicine, but, of course, it didn't taste like medicine. No, no, not at all. It was the best pie Mrs. Kozak had ever tasted—and the best I ever tasted, too, since I sneaked a little piece for myself when no one was looking. The crust was perfect, so delicate, yet not crumbly or dry, and it had a smooth texture and subtle taste all its own—and the pumpkin filling had a touch of fresh ginger to it, very subtle, very delicious, and good for the digestion."

"I'm glad you both liked it."

"We did, we really did—but you know, *Pani,* it made me think that your pies are so good that maybe someone could sell them to people."

"Really? Well, who would that someone be?"

"Why, me. You and I could start a partnership—a business partnership. I could sell your pies here in the market—we could set up a little space for you if, that is, you were ever interested in doing such a thing."

"Well, Mr. Kozak, it's an interesting proposition. How many pies would that mean? How many do you think you could sell in a day?"

"Easily five, maybe ten. People enjoy your pies. I've heard my customers talking about them, praising them to the heavens. You have quite a following already. I mean it's kind of a little joke in the neighborhood, isn't it? If you get sick, you can expect a pie from Mrs. Olszewska—it's an affectionate little joke, you see, very affectionate, of course."

"Well, Mr. Kozak, could you give me time to think it over?"

That night, when we were all together upstairs—she, me, invited to stay for dinner again, Mr. O. and, behind his door, Adam—she brought up Mr. Kozak's offer, explaining that it might be a way to make extra money and certainly a way to leave the dry cleaners—a true sweatshop even though the brothers who owned the place were decent men. Mr. O. was highly receptive to the idea, but it was clear Agnes still needed convincing. For one thing, she didn't like the idea of selling what she'd given away for years and years—an argument for which we had no answer. In fact, Mr. O. and I could only shrug our shoulders. For another thing, she worried that making pies every day might disrupt Adam's studies.

"Oh no," I piped in, "that wouldn't be a problem. You wouldn't disturb us at all."

Adam agreed from behind the door—causing Mrs. Olszewska to nod her head soberly. Then she smiled and disclosed that she'd already chosen a name for her business—Pie Man Pies, after the nursery rhyme Adam liked so much when he was little. We all agreed it was a fine name and Mrs. Olszewska sighed deeply and declared the matter settled.

The next afternoon, she called Mr. Kozak and said she would accept his offer. Mr. Kozak—maybe a little surprised that Mrs. Olszewska had taken him seriously—hemmed and hawed and hemmed and hawed and—finally regrouping—said he intended to charge three times what a bakery typically charged for a pie. The high price was justified, he added, because a bakery pie tasted like a bakery pie, while Mrs. Olszewska's pies were and tasted homemade—even better than homemade if such a thing were possible. Mrs. Olszewska asked about those people—old people mostly—who couldn't afford to pay and she and Mr. Kozak agreed that they would pay a small fraction of the price or even be given the pie for free.

Mr. Kozak told his new partner he had a friend in New Haven who would sell her pie tins at a good price. And boxes? Why bother? Instead, Mrs. Olszewska could wrap her pies in clear plastic bags, inserting a little card that identified the pies as hers—much cheaper that way. Later that afternoon, Mr. Kozak called back and said his brother-in-law—who owned Mike's Luncheonette downtown—was also interested in selling her pies. Mrs. Olszewska laughed out loud. She had doubled her business before she had even sold her first pie!

She then called Danuta and asked if she would be her partner and coworker in the new venture. Danuta agreed immediately, although she asked why her friend wanted her enterprise to be known as Pie Man Pies when she was a woman. Mrs. Olszewska explained that the name came from an American nursery rhyme—or maybe English. The next morning they met at the dry cleaners and gave the brothers two weeks' notice which, it turned out, wasn't necessary—business was slow anyway.

Mrs. Olszewska and Danuta immediately went to work getting their new enterprise in order. Mr. O. said that if his wife were going to hire Danuta as a partner and assistant, she might have to talk to a lawyer about employment taxes and other details—and he volunteered to do the research work himself. Mrs. Olszewska gave him a kiss. All she wanted to do was make the pies and keep the books—she was always good with numbers.

She ordered a few hundred pie tins from a Mr. Rosol in New Haven and several large rolls of perforated plastic bags. She ordered a hundred white boxes too—since a plastic bag would be disastrously messy with a cream pie—opting for the less expensive windowless variety. She decided to place the pie into the plastic bag, insert her business card into the bag, and on the card note what kind of pie it was—A for apple, B for blueberry, etc., etc.—then she would tie the plastic bag with a brilliant red ribbon. For cream and meringue pies, she would Scotch tape her card to the box after marking it with CC for custard cream, LM for lemon meringue, and so on.

Her cards read:

PIE MAN PIES
Agnes Olszewska
7 Peru Street
Silverton, Connecticut
BE7-0088

At seven o'clock in the morning on June 12, 1965, Mrs. Olszewska and Danuta Fiore began making Pie Man pies. The first batch was blueberry, the second cherry, the third Mrs. Olszewska's signature French apple with its fat, vanilla-soaked raisins and thick layer of vanilla icing—like hardened snow, Mr. O. liked to say, on a winter pond. Once the pies cooled, Mrs. Olszewska delivered them in her car to Mr. Kozak's market—and then downtown to Mike's Luncheonette. That winter, she bought a used van and Mr. O. devised an ingenious system of self-locking shelves to hold the precious cargo secure. While Mrs. Olszewska was delivering the pies, Danuta remained at 7 Peru Street cleaning up the kitchen. When the boss returned before noon, the two friends had lunch—usually outside or in the kitchen, rarely upstairs with Adam and me. They chatted for hours sometimes in their odd mixture of Polish and English: about the business, Danuta's new husband—the handsome Sgt. Alfredo Fiore—Adam's education, and a host of other topics. It was easy to see there weren't two happier people on earth. Danuta said that working with Mrs. Olszewska turned any job into play. And it was a joy for Adam and me to hear them—a pleasant chirping punctuated now and then by Danuta's shrieks of laughter. They acted like two teenage girls sometimes—giggling at private jokes and double entendres, intended or not, funny or not. They were both shareholders in PMP and made more money—even at the outset—than they had ever earned at the dry cleaners. And Mrs. Olszewska trusted her friend completely. She shared with her all her secrets—including baking secrets—even how to make her fabulous crusts.

The two friends soon settled into an efficient work routine. The emergencies and surprises that had marked the first weeks of PMP became less dire and threatening—and soon vanished altogether. In the fall, the Polish Home in Hartford became their third customer—asking for five pies a day. Then BJ's Cafe, Sal's Deli, the Silver Diner on the turnpike, and the University Diner in Middletown put in their orders and, by Thanksgiving, Pie Man Pies was making more than fifty pies a day! At that point, Mr. O. installed two extra ovens in the kitchen and Mr. Laver—a retired trucker and Teamster organizer who lived on Canada Street—was hired to deliver the goods.

Mrs. Olszewska understood that the three ovens were necessary for the success of her business, but her beautiful kitchen—with its work island and birch table, its handsome cabinets and shelved pantry—had lost its charm, had given over completely to the business of making, baking, and delivering pies. The room was littered with stacks of tins and boxes, bags of flour, tubs of lard, and God knows what else. On the work island were freakishly large bowls in which Mrs. Olszewski mixed the crust ingredients. From seven in the morning until three or four in the afternoon, the kitchen was an absolute disaster.

The women settled on a system that kept the production flow at a steady rate. Mrs. Olszewska made the crust, but Danuta actually formed the pies—she could lay down a crust, bottom and top, and then flute the edges in four minutes flat. Either woman made the filling, first slathering apricot preserve over the crust—one of Mrs. Olszewska's many secrets. As the cold weather set in, Pie Man Pies was doing better than anyone had expected or imagined. People raved about the pies and—as Mr. Kozak had predicted—they didn't mind the higher prices and only a few customers—an ancient *babcia* or two—accepted Mr. Kozak's generous discount. Not a single customer accepted a free pie—that would be charity, after all. It was a very busy time—and with Christmas coming, we all suspected it would only get busier.

10

IN DECEMBER, DANUTA STARTED ACTING strangely. She moped around the kitchen—frowning, growling, and acting like a morose schoolgirl. When Mrs. Olszewska asked her what was wrong, Danuta started to tear up and announced that she had a confession to make—she was pregnant.

"But that's good news," Mrs. Olszewska said, kissing the tears from her friend's eyes. "Why are you crying? Why are you behaving like a goose?"

Danuta took a deep breath and said she was crying because instead of making pies she'd be home raising her baby—she pronounced it *bibby*. Sgt. Alfredo wanted her to be a full-time mom—and so did she—but she didn't want to abandon Mrs. Olszewska, especially with the business doing so well. Mrs. Olszewska said that didn't matter. Danuta could go on maternity leave or be paid a partial salary or whatever until the child was old enough and Danuta could return to work. Mrs. Olszewska tried to get her friend to stop crying—but Danuta blubbered away all morning and stopped only when Mrs. Olszewska told her she was ruining the crusts by making them salty with her tears.

In January, Mrs. Olszewska hired two teenage girls—both from Poland—to replace Danuta, who planned on leaving PMP sometime in the early spring. Mr. O. found the girls cleaning offices in the Aircraft's engineering department, working for a company in Hartford that had—through special visas—brought them into the USA, paid them considerably less than minimum wage, and put them up in a cheap hotel room in the city—which they had to pay for out of their own already meager earnings. Mrs. Olszewska told her husband to make them an offer, promising not only to pay them much more than what they were earning, but also to contribute toward the rent for the rooms above Mr. Kozak's market—which Mr. and Mrs. Kozak and Wanda had finally vacated. Excited at the prospect of sending more money to their families overseas, the girls readily agreed, but when they gave notice, the owner of the cleaning company—a real pig—refused to let them go. He complained that Mr. O. had no right to hire away his "Polack girls" and threatened to bring suit against Pie Man Pies—now incorporated, as advised by Mr. O.'s Hartford attorney. Mr. O. spoke to the vice president at the Aircraft who had hired the cleaning company in the first place and—miracle of miracles—the suit was dropped and the owner was profusely apologetic, offering up the two girls to Pie Man Pies as if he were giving them away as brides.

Both girls were thin, although not nearly as thin as yours truly. Slaving away at the cleaning company, they'd sent their families whatever money they could eke out—and often that meant going without food. The older girl, Helena, barely spoke English. She was very pretty, though, and nimble with her fingers, so she worked with Danuta rolling out, forming, and fluting pie crusts. The other girl, Elzbieta, who wanted to be called Betsy, a more American name—which she, Helena, and Danuta all pronounced as *Bid-zee*—wasn't unattractive, she was just indifferent to how she looked. Betsy and I soon became friends. She was intelligent, a quick study, and her English was excellent. She became my second, unofficial tutee.

On their first day of work, Mrs. Olszewska introduced Helena and Betsy to Adam. They became visibly nervous—my talking to the door made their eyes bug out. Helena starting shaking and didn't stop until twenty or so minutes later. Betsy, while not distraught, was very suspicious and wary. She whispered to me that Adam must be "a crazy boy" to be kept in a closet all his life. Later, when Betsy became my de facto student, she no longer shied away from Adam's door and had no problem carrying on conversations with him, some quite lengthy. Helena never once spoke to him—and rarely spoke of him. One time Adam told Betsy that she could read any book she wanted from his library and, in fact, one day he left a pile of books in the hallway for her. On the top of the pile was *Jane Eyre*—leading Betsy to believe that the strange young man upstairs somehow knew what she was thinking on the day they first met. Most of the books, though, were by American writers, since he knew how much Betsy wanted to be an American girl.

Adam, the Benthamic spy, kept his eye on both Betsy and Helena, but it was Betsy who interested him—and me—more. When Betsy started night school, Adam and I helped with her studies. She met with us in the hallway—she was given her own school desk, I don't know where Mr. O. got them—during her lunch hour to prepare for class or study for an exam or just chat. The hour became part of Adam's curriculum—a seminar in whatever subject Betsy was studying at the time. He and I thought Betsy would get her high school equivalency diploma in two or three years. It took her one.

Helena had absolutely no interest in school or learning and so had no interest in Adam whatsoever. She never thought of Adam as a harmless boy or a hermit pure of heart, she just thought he was nuts—or else a kind of malevolent spirit, a poltergeist or something. Helena was so attractive and sexy and had so many boys interested in her she never had to work for anything. While Betsy went to night classes, Helena was out at the movies or at a dance or at a restaurant. Helena was vain and loved being flattered, but she was untrusting and in control and—as far as Betsy or anyone else knew—she never surrendered her virtue to some local Don Juan. Mrs. Olszewska thought Helena was sweet like a child, but also petulant and self-centered. The truth was—for all the attention young men paid to her and all the socializing she did—she was a lonely young woman who longed for her family overseas. The only thing that mattered to her was sending money home—and that she did religiously, giving up virtually every penny she earned. Aside from the rent, which was modest and partly subsidized by Pie Man Pies, she had virtually no expenses. She didn't spend much money on food because boys were always taking her out to dinner or giving her chocolates or fruit baskets or cheeses and other gourmet delicacies—and Helena was more than happy to share her spoils with Betsy and the rest of us at 7 Peru Street.

11

IN MAY 1966, DANUTA LEFT WORK TO SPEND HER final month of pregnancy at home. She wanted to continue in the kitchen with Agnieszka and the girls—but hubby Alfredo said it was high time *she* was waited on and treated like a queen. Alfredo also confided to Mrs. Olszewska that if they had a girl they were going to name the child after her—and sure enough on June 9, at six in the morning little Agnieszka was born. Mrs. Olszewska saw her namesake in the delivery room and for a few brief moments held her in her arms.

Then something terrible happened—something no one could foresee or prevent or even in the end understand. At three in the afternoon, Mrs. Olszewska came home from the hospital to tell Adam and me—in the middle of a hallway lesson—that little Agnieszka was dead.

"There's no use asking questions," she said, "because I have no answers."

Oh, it was awful. For an instant, the world was overcome by utter and complete darkness. Nothing lived, nothing moved. My knees were so shaky I could barely get out of my school desk. But Mrs. Olszewska was even worse. I'd never seen her so distraught and saddened. Her skin seemed to hang from her bones, softening, turning into a grotesque jelly. Her eyes were red and bulging. The collar of her white blouse was gray with tears—hers and Danuta's. Then she collapsed in a heap on the hallway floor, hanging on to the knob of Adam's door. A minute or two later, when she regained consciousness, she looked into my eyes—I was holding her in my arms—and she smiled and laughed a small whispery laugh. Then she sighed and shook her head no and said she was going to bed. She had already called Mr. O. from the hospital and he was on his way home. In fact, as she spoke, he was running up the stairs. Before he reached us, Mrs. Olszewska asked me to call Helena and Betsy—who had left an hour or two before—to tell them there would be no work the next day, and probably not for the remainder of the week.

"People can go without pie for a while," she said.

When Mr. O. took his wife to bed, I remained in the hallway sitting in my school desk. Adam was completely silent, which came as no surprise to me—that was his usual reaction to anything out of the ordinary. But as I started to go home he spoke. I could tell he was very close to the door, touching it, I guessed, with his forehead and talking loudly and angrily into the wood. He wondered why there would be such a thing as a life that didn't last longer than a day. What was the point? Little Agnieszka's life was a glimmer of light—the quick flash of an instamatic—except not terribly bright at all. More like a flash seen underwater. He said he felt queasy and dizzy. What was it about this all-too-brief life that disturbed him so much? It wasn't like the loss of a young adult or a child. It wasn't even worth an accompanying irony—just a matter of time misplaced and misused, a journey started without the first step taken. The infant had gained nothing in its few hours of existence and so nothing really had been lost. There had been no investment in that little life, just the vague idea of a make-believe life, a tacked-on life, a life that was barely more than the word *life*.

The next several days Mrs. Olszewska spent with Danuta and Alfredo, first at the hospital, then at their home on Finland Street. When she returned each evening she was exhausted by the physical demands of her own grief. Mr. O. picked up pizza from the Little Rendezvous Apizza each night and the three of us sat in the hallway with Adam on the other side of his door eating plain pizza—no toppings, mozzarella, double dough. Alfredo and Danuta decided they would not have a wake, just a funeral Mass at St. Paul's, followed by a small reception at the K-Club for family and friends.

I went to the service with Mr. O. and Mrs. Olszewska and then to the brunch at the K-Club. Adam, of course, stayed in his room. It was quite a spread—long tables covered with brown butcher paper, urns of coffee, Viennese pastries, rye bread, slices of ham rolled into perfect tubes, bland mazowiecki cheese in neat shingles, bricks of butter, bowls of cream or sugar, metal juice pitchers weeping cold tears, paper napkins, and stacks of paper coffee cups. I wondered if it was all too much, but it really wasn't—grief needs to be fed or else it'll never go away. At the service, people seemed to be in a trance, stunned and numb and incredulous. But when they got to the K-Club, they talked, socialized, ate, drank coffee or something from the bar—Mr. O. bought me one highball, then another, and then a third. Quite tipsy, I returned to 7 Peru Street around two thirty and sat outside Adam's door, not even letting him know I was there.

A week or so after the funeral service for little Agnieszka, I came to work as usual only to discover a manila envelope on the seat of my school desk. I opened the package and discovered a roll of 8mm film. By the stairwell I saw an 8mm projector. I recognized it as Agnes's—she had months before shown me her home movies of her baby Adam, as well as that sad, haunting, painful-to-watch footage shot by Dr. Cohen of Adam's bloody nose and scream after Mr. O. had carried him—for the briefest of seconds—into the outside world.

But this was no home movie. It was a kind of visual poem—with little Agnieszka as the subject.

"Can you operate the projector?" Adam asked. I said I could, and when I finished threading the film, I was told to turn off the overhead light and project the images onto a little home movie screen at the end of the hallway, which Mr. O. apparently had set up early in the morning—certainly Adam wouldn't have ventured for that long out of his room. He said he had made the movie himself using his mother's old 8mm camera. Mr. O. had had the film developed and found Adam an old editing device, a track with sprockets, and a cheesy plastic monitor that allowed him to see what he'd shot frame by frame. Mr. O. also got him splicing tape from a downtown camera supply store.

The portrait of little Agnieszka began with five minutes of utter blackness, then a few seconds of a blurry still of a pregnant woman's stomach—taken from a magazine advertisement—then a few seconds of his bedroom lamp filmed through a glass of murky water, then a few seconds of cartoon mice shot directly from the TV screen, then five more minutes of blackness.

That was it—I didn't know what to make of it. It was abstract and kind of remote and unfeeling and eerie. The womb, the light of birth, the cartoon of a childhood that never was—all that I had no problem understanding, but it was the pair of darknesses—so long and so tedious—that I found disturbing. Yes, the darknesses made me think about what had really taken place—they actually seemed as long as the infinities they represented—but it was a lot to ask of a would-be viewer to sit through them. Then Adam asked if he should give the film to Danuta as a gift—a remembrance—and I said it probably wouldn't be a good idea, she probably wouldn't understand, and it might make her feel worse rather than better. I waited for a response from Adam but there wasn't any. I told them I'd show the movie to his parents. No response this time either. He had become the quiet Adam again.

As I had expected, Adam's film completely baffled Mr. O. and Mrs. Olszewska.

"It's mostly just blackness," Mrs. Olszewska said. "It's like my camera wasn't working or maybe Adam put the film in wrong or something."

"I think it's supposed to be symbolic," Mr. O. replied.

"What does that mean, symbolic?"

"I think it's supposed to be a flicker of light surrounded by two darknesses. Just like little Agnieszka's life. Don't you see?"

Mrs. Olszewska nodded her head—a quick irritated nod—and said someone—meaning me—should have explained that to her before she sat down to watch the thing. It would have helped knowing what she was looking at—she wouldn't have been so confused and annoyed.

When I asked if we should show the film to Danuta and her husband, she said no. There was no hesitation on her part

"She'd just think we were making fun of her. Even if you explained what it meant she wouldn't understand. She's not a weak person. She's seen death before. But this would just confuse her. I know this tragedy has affected Adam and I know this movie is from his heart. And he's right, he's right. Little Agnieszka was just a little light and nothing more. But I can just see Danuta's face, looking around the room with that bewildered look of hers. It would be a cruel thing to do—it would just cause her pain. You'll tell Adam, won't you? Or should I?"

"No, I'll tell him."

And I did that afternoon. The next morning when I went to work there was a large cardboard box in the middle of the hallway—and in it was stuffed the 8mm camera and its set of lights, the projector, the rolled-up screen, the editing device, editing tape, and boxes of unused film.

Well, I thought, so much for Adam's career as a filmmaker.

That film of his really wasn't what I'd call a cinematic masterpiece, but it bothered me nonetheless—and for a long time afterward. It seemed so cold and analytical. It really didn't take into account Danuta's and Alfredo's feelings—or anyone else's. It was more like a philosophical treatise in visual terms. And yet, I couldn't be critical of its author—it was a response, a reaction. It must have been prompted by some sympathetic impulse, some feeling and emotion. It showed in some way I couldn't exactly explain that Adam had a heart.

One night I dreamed I was showing Adam's film in the Olszewski living room. Everyone was there—Mrs. Olszewska, Mr. O., Danuta,

Alfredo, Helena and Betsy, Mrs. Wrobel—except Adam, of course. And everyone was dressed in black and seated on folding chairs. I gave a little talk—explaining what the darknesses meant, what the blurry light meant, and what the cartoon mice meant. I signaled Mr. O. and the lights went out and the projector went on—but the screen, of course, was completely dark. Alfredo lit up a cigarette and the tiny red glow became a kind of beacon for the rest of us during the first "infinity"—then came the light and the mice, almost blinding compared to the pitch blackness that preceded it—and made misty and mysterious by Sgt. Fiore's cigarette smoke curling in the projector's light. Suddenly, I thought I saw a face behind the screen. It looked like Mrs. Olszewska on her way to and from the kitchen for some reason. Then the second "infinity" passed by and when that was done, the screen turned white, the film sounded like a fish flip-flopping as it finished passing through the projector gate, and Mr. O. put on the lights. And there, standing in front of the screen, was a dark, handsome young man with long black hair and a shadowy near-beard. Danuta gasped—a great swallow of air. Mrs. Wrobel screamed softly. Sgt. Fiore stood up, ready to defend his wife—and the rest of us, for that matter. Mrs. Olszewska remained in her chair, silent, mouth open, lower lip trembling.

"Who are you?" Danuta called out.

"Madam," the beautiful young man said laughing, "I'm Adam."

12

THERE WERE OTHER DREAMS, DOZENS OF THEM, in which I saw Adam's face—always a handsome face, if a bit too pale and with features a bit too fine and almost feminine—framed by luxuriant black hair and the beginnings of a beard. On what did I—more exactly, my subconscious—base this face? Beats me. Maybe I'd watched too many Bela Lagosi movies or something because my dream-Adam had a vampirish quality to him. Was it based on anything real, a glimpse of him as he picked up his dinner or stared out his bedroom window at the walkway? No. Nothing of the kind. My idea of Adam was based on the stuff dreams are made of.

One dream in particular was very sexy. I dreamed it during one of the worst heat waves on record. Those weeks were a terrible time at 7 Peru Street. While the house didn't allow in much sunlight, it also didn't allow any kind of circulation, so the air quickly turned syrupy—and there was no air conditioning. Mrs. Olszewska didn't believe in it; she thought it was good to sweat and so she and Danuta and those poor Polish girls nearly evaporated away each day making pies in the kitchen. There were fans—antique slo-mo things—placed in every corner of the house, but they didn't help much. They just moved the hot, humid air in useless circles. On the night of what turned out to be the hottest of all those hot nights, I went home after dinner and as soon as I got there I collapsed on my bed and fell asleep. I dreamed—almost immediately—that I was sitting in my usual spot in the hallway reading from some book, sweat dripping from my face—there was a heat wave in my dream, too. Mrs. Olszewska, the Polish girls, and Danuta were baking pies downstairs, but were unusually quiet—it was too hot to talk. I wore a delicate white sun dress. It was supposed to help me stay cool—but it didn't help at all. A fan behind me at the top of the stairs was more like a blast from a furnace than a breeze off the ocean. My dress was soon marked by sweat stains, circles under the arms and a soggy triangle at the collarbone. I hiked the dress up to the top of my thighs, trying to air myself out. Then I just took the thing off. A minute later I removed my bra and stuffed it into my pocketbook. Then I slipped off my shoes. Then I took off my panties. The air from the old fan suddenly felt cool and my skin tingled. I realized I was floating above my school desk. I was gliding slowly toward the door and then *I went right through it* as if it were a kind of membrane. I continued floating a foot or so off the ground and bumped into Adam's thigh. He looked the same as he did in my other dream—except he was also naked and he was waiting for me. My right foot touched his left calf and moved slowly up to his crotch. His skin was hot and slippery. The air in the room—no fan there, either—got hotter and thicker. The shade was completely drawn and the sunlight was like a huge burning beast trying to force its way inside. My dream-Adam put his face between my legs—the heat of his breath was hotter than the fan air. I began to squirm, my rear moving in small circles. Finally, his mouth opened. I felt his tongue—it was like a little fish.

13

JAKE GLOWAC WAS ADAM'S FIRST AND, FOR A LONG time, only friend, although it was clear from the outset they had nothing in common and didn't particularly like each other that much either. When he was a toddler—and moved freely throughout the world outside his bedroom—Adam was clumsy and uncoordinated, while Jake—more than a year older—was rough, agile, strong, a boy who thrived on competition. For a while, he served as Adam's protector, but it really wasn't his idea. According to Mrs. Olszewska, Jakes's mother had asked him to watch over Adam and he couldn't refuse her.

When Adam decided never to leave his room, Jake was the only friend allowed to continue his visits. He came by two or three times a year, always to play chess. I'd see him in the hallway—he was there at four o'clock usually—studying the chess board and pieces Mrs. Olszewska had set up on an ancient, scarred end table from Mr. O.'s workshop. Adam had his chess board on the other side of the door—and they called out their moves to each other. Adam wasn't a bad player—but he wasn't nearly so aggressive as Jake, so he never came out on top. Now and then I'd meet Mrs. Glowac at Kozak's Market and one time she told me she had asked her son to let Adam win at chess just once—but Jake had adamantly refused—he was that competitive! But Adam never seemed to mind losing at chess. It was a game he didn't care about—too linear and slow to develop, he said—although he did wish now and then that Jake would participate in an activity *he* enjoyed like drawing pictures or listening to music—or just talking about things. But Jake played chess and that was that.

During high school, Jake had become a popular and supremely confident young man. He seemed to excel in everything. Mr. and Mrs. Olszewski didn't like Jake and thought he was a conceited brat—Mr. O. called him Golden Boy—but they allowed him into their house because they thought Adam enjoyed his company. Adam, on the other hand, tolerated Jake because he thought his parents liked him and wanted them to be pals. When the truth finally came out after dinner one time as to how everyone really felt about Jake, Adam and Mr. O. and I had a good laugh—but Mrs. Olszewska wasn't amused at all.

"Sometimes," she said, "we're just too polite."

In 1967, Jake made his biannual visit a week before Christmas and, as always, he insisted on playing chess. Adam hadn't improved his game one bit—but he devised a devious strategy that promised to give himself a victory after all those years of defeat. He called it the Odysseus-Achilles Strategy and it was designed to use Jake's blind competitiveness against himself.

Jake arrived at four as usual. I was staying for dinner that night and was busy helping Mrs. Olszewska in the kitchen. When Jake came in through the back door, she greeted him with a friendly hello and asked if he'd like a piece of pie from the day's production—Danuta and the girls had just left work—to which Jake, lifting his right hand, said no, he didn't want to spoil his supper. He went upstairs where a table with a chess board and pieces awaited him.

In the first game—he reported to me later on—Adam played so impulsively and so carelessly and so stupidly that Jake complained he wasn't even trying—but Adam feigned innocence—and ignorance—secretly delighted that the strategy seemed to be working. He was the cunning Odysseus and Jake was the blustering, raging, ultimately impotent Achilles. Jake complained and protested—bellowing his displeasure—but he couldn't resist playing again and again—he was addicted to winning, he had to tally victory after victory—no matter how tainted. Meanwhile, Adam sat back in his chair behind the door—or so he said—inventing spurious defenses and mad assaults—refusing to take enemy pieces and giving up his own in orgies of self-sacrifice.

Jake finally left in a huff. When I went upstairs, I gave the secret knock and Adam, laughing like an idiot, related every detail of the games—there were ten in all. He had turned victory into something frivolous and stupid. It was that evening when we all met in the hallway that we confessed our true feelings about Jake Glowac, and he was never invited to visit again—nor did he ever ask to drop by.

14

I WAS TOLD THAT CHRISTMAS HAD ALWAYS BEEN a wonderful time at 7 Peru Street. Early on, before Adam went to school, Mrs. Olszewska worked for days to create a magnificent feast—mushroom soup, beet soup, rows of pierogies, carp with cucumber sauce and, even though the traditional Christmas Eve vigil was supposed to be meat-free, Mrs. Olszewska, not one for religious niceties, also served *golabki*, different kinds of sausage—Mr. O. was in heaven—a roasted chicken, and a beautiful ham. Following that were varieties of—what else?—pies. Usually Adam's grandparents came down for the party—plus Mrs. Wrobel and her daughter Angela—before she left for California. It was also traditional to leave an extra place setting in case an unexpected guest dropped by.

On Christmas Eve Mrs. Olszewska—normally a frugal woman—insisted that every light be turned on so the house could become a beacon for anyone wandering in the night. Adam later said that the house enjoyed being a beacon—a lighthouse—a house of light!

When Adam started living in his room, Mrs. Olszewska told me she brought the party to him. And after the grandparents followed each other to the grave in 1962 and 1963—it was just Mr. O. and Mrs. Olszewska and, on the other side of the door, Adam. Mrs. Wrobel, with her daughter gone, spent the holidays with her sister in New Haven.

Mrs. Olszewska still made her typical feast. Mr. O. built a long narrow table—and on it Mrs. Olszewska draped an elegant tablecloth and placed candles and beautiful serving dishes containing her culinary masterpieces. Then the parents would leave and the son would open the door and serve himself. A little later, the parents returned, sat down, and had dinner conversing with Adam through the ever-present door.

When Mrs. Olszewska began Pie Man Pies, the Christmas Eve dinner for three became kind of an office Christmas Eve party. It started downstairs—Danuta and Alfredo were there, plus my pop and I, Helena and Betsy, Mr. Laver the driver, Mrs. Wrobel—her sister had passed—but at dinnertime the entire party shifted upstairs where the table had been set up and we somehow squeezed in around it. We looked like a scene from a Marx Brothers movie. Adam—who had already taken his food and drink (vodka and honey liqueur and blackberry brandy) into his room before the crowd was allowed upstairs—was very much in the holiday spirit and chatted with people through the door, often shouting to be heard above the din. The only one who didn't chat with him was Helena. She stayed at the edge of the crowd near the top of the stairs—ready to take off if something weird happened. The party lasted until nine o'clock when everyone—including dearest pop—was pretty much wasted. As the party broke up, Adam sang "O Holy Night" in such a lovely lilting tenor that Danuta and Mrs. Olszewska couldn't hold back tears.

15

IN 1966—WHEN ADAM WAS 16 AND I HAD BEEN HIS tutor for two years—he began to write poetry, gothic, recklessly satirical poetry, sometimes verging on the hysterical—although underlying all of it was his Benthamic generosity, his insistence on the greatest good for all always. Finally, two submissions were published—one in a journal called *Snakebite* put out by a small college in New Mexico, the other by a journal in Ohio called *In Free,* which had a policy of not rejecting any submissions. Then Adam submitted to a journal called *The Letter C*—published out of UCLA. The editor, he told me, was none other than Mrs. B.—his tutor for two days—and my predecessor. Adam's submission was returned a week after he had mailed it out. The poems went unmarked, untouched and—it seemed—unread. With them he found a rejection slip on which Mrs. B. had written in pencil:

> One can't write about the world
> unless one lives in it.
> Sorry to disappoint, Adam, but no.
> My best to your mother.

After a while he stopped submitting his poems and by 1967 had given up writing poetry for good.

16

IT OCCURRED TO DEAREST ADAM A MONTH OR SO after his sixteenth birthday that he should begin a journal. He preferred journal to diary, since diary—despite Mr. Pepys—sounded girlish and giggly. Of course, he wanted to begin with a memorable entry—something witty and profound—but nothing, he said, came to him. Anyway, what could he possibly write about?

"You know," he said, "it's really stupid for a recluse to keep a journal. One entry would be almost exactly like all the others."

I told him that the future—even some small part of it—should know that one Adam Olszewski had walked the earth, that he had longings and misgivings and beliefs, that he had wished for this and was critical of that, and that he was a young man of some worldliness even though he had no worldly experience.

There was a silence. Then he laughed and we went on to something else.

17

AROUND THIS TIME BUSINESS BEGAN TO PICK UP for Pie Man Pies. The pies were popular in small independent markets and diners between Hartford and Middletown and were making headway into New Haven. With Pie Man Pies, small retailers could offer something the big stores couldn't—something truly homemade. Eventually, Mrs. Olszewska decided to make some marketing changes. Now every pie came in a white box with the words

PIE MAN PIES

printed in bold red letters across the top. Beneath the name was a plastic window through which the customer could see the pie in all its glory and—under the window, also in red ink—was a line-art portrait of the Pie Man himself, a moonfaced man wearing a floppy toque. Under the face was a single word

HOMEMADE

and—in tiny print at the bottom—Pie Man Pies, 7 Peru Street, Silverton, Connecticut. The Pie Man image was also stamped into the bottom of each aluminum pie plate.

If, at first, the image looked like Adam as a boy that's because it was. Mrs. Olszewska's found it in her collection of Adammemorabilia—one of the few self-portraits he had ever drawn. He was in first grade at the time and drawing self-portraits was part of an art project—but it really wasn't a proper self-portrait at all, just a few disdainful, impatient lines. But Mrs. Olszewska realized that a boy baker with a moony face made absolutely no sense, so she brought the original drawing to a commercial artist named Eduardo who, with a few more bold strokes, made the Pie Man appear grown up—and then added the chef's hat and then sent it, with Mrs. Olszewska's blessing, to the printer who applied it to the box and pie plate and eventually to posters and T-shirts and other promotional items. The jolly Pie Man face also appeared in bright red on the new white delivery truck Mr. O. had procured from somewhere for some ridiculously low price. It was very ironic I thought—as did Adam when I mentioned it to him—that that big white delivery truck was seen by hundreds or even thousands every day—and on it was a huge representation of a hermit who hadn't stepped into the public world for nearly a decade.

18

SOMEONE SUGGESTED TO MRS. OLSZEWSKA THAT she put up a sign somewhere designating 7 Peru Street as the home of Pie Man Pies. It seemed like a good idea—good advertising and public relations and so on—and even Adam said he thought the house wouldn't mind being so decorated. But Mrs. Olszewska said no. She was very sensitive to the fact that her business was right in the middle of a neighborhood—and she wanted more than anything to keep a low profile. She instructed Mr. Laver to park his delivery truck in her driveway rather than on Peru—a very narrow residential street—where it might cause traffic problems. She also didn't want her girls to play their music at a volume that might disturb the neighbors—and she asked them to be as inconspicuous as possible when they ate their lunches in the back yard or walked down Peru Street to spend their lunch hours in the park.

For Mrs. Olszewska, a big sign that read PIE MAN PIES over the front door of the house was out of the question. Danuta argued that Mr. Kozak's grocery had a sign over its front door and that was a business that was right in the middle of a residential neighborhood—but Mrs. Olszewska wouldn't accept the analogy. Mr. Kozak's was a retail business—people went to his establishment to buy things. Pie Man Pie was not a business in that way. Nothing was sold at 7 Peru Street. It was where the pies were made—and that made all the difference in the world.

As a compromise Mrs. Olszewska had a small sign made for the back door—the door that led into the kitchen. It contained The Pie Man's image—the revised and artistically aged image of young, moonfaced Adam—and above it, in red, the words PIE MAN PIES—and below, also in red, it said HOMEMADE.

19

EVERYONE THOUGHT HELENA WOULD MARRY some handsome wealthy young American boy and live the life of a pampered wife in an affluent suburb—but one day she up and left for home. She had stayed away from her family long enough—or so she wrote in a note to Betsy—and while she enjoyed working for Mrs. Olszewska and Danuta, and enjoyed living with Betsy, and enjoyed being taken out on dates by so many handsome young men—her homesickness had become overwhelming. It was by then a physical illness—a series of unbearably sharp pains in her stomach accompanied by a nausea that never really went away. She left in early May 1967 without telling anyone—not even Betsy. She bought her plane ticket, paid her bills, collected her things, packed her suitcases and—on a humid evening while Betsy was in class—vanished. One of her boyfriends gave her a ride to the airport. She didn't leave a forwarding address, but insinuated that she would get in touch with everyone in the future. She never did—and no one ever knew what became of her. Betsy tried to contact Helena's family in the old country, but she received no reply to her letters and post cards and eventually stopped sending them.

Danuta and Betsy easily managed the workload in Helena's absence, but Mrs. Olszewska worried that by August of that year they would be overwhelmed with new business. But just as Mrs. Olszewska decided to put a classified ad in the newspaper, Mr. Kozak called and wondered—since he'd noticed one of his boarders had gone—if Agnes would hire his daughter to take her place. Maybe part-time to start, he said, and if it didn't work out, it didn't work out. Wanda had just turned eighteen and had adamantly refused to work for her father who—settled now in the suburbs—was looking to retire. He was hoping his daughter would take over his business, but she had no interest in or talent for tending a market. She hated the place, the meats, the sausages, the flypaper, the penny candies, the canned goods. Most of all, she hated the resident odors—dried mushrooms, marjoram, old garlic—which I always kind of liked.

Later that week she visited Mrs. Olszewska and sat for an interview in the parlor. She was pretty enough—with straight honey blonde hair and a flawless milky complexion—but she was such an odd duck, such a strange, disconnected girl. She shuffled her feet when she walked, she slouched in her chair and—most disconcerting of all to Mrs. Olszewska—she mumbled. And when she laughed—always nervously—it was through her teeth—a hissing that sounded like a tea kettle. Mrs. Olszewska asked her to talk about herself and she barely progressed beyond her name. And to more direct questions all the girl could say was "I don't know" or "I'm not sure." Wanda seemed to be a young woman without any interests—not in schoolwork, not in sports, not in socializing with friends, not in boys. She lived with her parents in their new suburban home and refused to take any steps toward independence. She was, Adam and I thought, something of a lump—but we understood that because her father was a former neighbor and a business partner, Mrs. Olszewska would hire her—and she did, as a part-timer. Still,the next day she submitted her ad for full-time help.

Wanda wasn't a great worker—but she wasn't a terrible one, either. She did what she was asked to do—no more, no less—and she was insanely quiet. She never spoke unless someone spoke to her and then only a few words. When it was time for her break, she didn't go outside for some fresh air, but went into the den and watched TV. I assumed she was a devotee of some soap opera or quiz show—but I noticed that at a given time she watched different shows—which led me to believe that it didn't matter what she watched just so long as she was watching something. I also noticed that the only time Wanda came to life was when I talked about Adam. Then she talked—asking question after question about the young man who locked himself in his room. Adam was a mystery to her—he was to all of us—but Wanda had a nagging curiosity about him—everyone else was invisible to her.

When the Italian girls began working in the kitchen, Wanda faded into the background even more—which she didn't mind in the least. A week after she hired Wanda, Mrs. Olszewska hired Anna Maria and Sophia—sisters, separated by a year. Their parents were friendly with Danuta's husband. Anna Maria and Sophia were smart, attractive girls—although neither was as stunning as Helena or as bright as Betsy. Danuta was very fond of them, especially Sophia—whom she renamed Zosia. Everyone in the house saw that Danuta and her Zosia were forming a special bond. Zosia was always cracking jokes and teasing everyone—and when Danuta learned that Zosia shared the same birthday as her poor infant Agnieszka, she practically adopted the girl on the spot. It had been over a year since she had lost her baby and she had more or less returned to her normal, playful, boisterous self, but there were still moments when she was a "sad bird," as Mrs. Olszewska called her—when her voice faded to a whisper or a few melancholy notes, when she drifted away, staring blankly out a window or at a pie crust that needed fluting. But Zosia cheered her up and while she was probably the laziest girl in the group, less eager to work than even Wanda—Mrs. Olszewska liked her the best because she was so much fun to be around and because she had—maybe once and for all—lifted Danuta out of the darkness of her great loss.

That August, Mrs. Olszewska's prediction of doubling or tripling PMP sales volume turned out to be wrong—she had been too conservative. The work day in the kitchen went from seven to five or six—often later. For the first time since PMP began, Mr. O. came home from the Aircraft to find his house filled with the bustle of women and the aromas of pies baking. When he walked into the kitchen, he gave his wife a kiss and said hello to Danuta and the girls, then he went upstairs to visit Adam and me—if, that is, I was staying for dinner. He liked sitting in the hallway with us, listening to our give and take, sometimes offering an opinion or a relevant anecdote of his own—but mostly just listening. His son, I told him, was making wonderful progress as a scholar. At seventeen, he was studying at a graduate-school level and was nearly fluent in Latin, French, and Polish.

But that was just what I told Mr. O. For me personally, Adam's education had become problematic. He had, years before, surpassed me in every subject (except music)—and had in effect become his tutor's tutor. And while Mrs. Olszewska said it was my companionship—and Adam's happiness—that really mattered, she also knew Adam's education was headed nowhere. Clearly, he wasn't going to leave home and attend college. More important, Adam never thought of himself as a young man preparing for a profession. His artwork and poems were only amusements for him—dilettante stuff. He had a profound love of learning, but it wasn't focussed and had no target—no discernible end. I told Mrs. Olszewska that—once I left—since I wasn't going to stay there forever—Adam should either have a tutor with a laundry list of advanced degrees or he should have no one at all. After the three of us discussed the matter one summer night we decided it probably ought to be no one at all.

20

ONE DAY—IT WAS IN APRIL 1970—I LOOKED AT A calendar and realized I had been Adam's tutor for nearly six years—and most of that time I'd barely been a tutor at all, more of a co-learner and friend. I was—as they say in the teaching profession—burned out. I had pretty much had it with that hallway—those walls—that school desk, that damn door—and though I learned from Adam and loved him and considered him my best friend—I thought it was time to move on. For years I'd been open about my plans to start a music and dance studio for children. Adam had already given it a Ravelian name—the Mother Goose Academy of Music and Dance—and I'd already picked out my ideal location—The House of Tong, a former Chinese restaurant in Middletown. Still, it was slow going. Although Mrs. Olszewska paid a salary commensurate with the local public school scale—it was really only a teacher's salary, after all, and without the summer vacation. That January, my pop cashed in most of his investments—Aircraft stock—and handed it over to yours truly so I could be the headmistress of my own school.

I left 7 Peru Street in June and started accepting students at the Mother Goose School in August. Adam was sad to see me go and—although he tried his best not to sound concerned and heartbroken—he was concerned and heartbroken. So was I, of course. During our last weeks together there were times when we were so sad we could barely talk. I'd still be nearby, I said, living with my pop—and I promised to call and keep him up to date on the school's progress, and maybe, maybe, if Adam ever decided to leave his room and his house, he could visit and watch my students practice their *pliés* or their Czerny. I promised to write—to keep in touch, to be close at hand. I took out a lease on The House of Tong and that summer my pop—assisted by Mr. O. and their Aircraft friends—ripped down the luxuriant red-and-gold wallpaper, replaced the bar with a barre, soundproofed practice rooms, and painted the walls pure white so they—unlike the rooms at

7 Peru Street—invited the light in and kept it there. Even after I left, I was still a frequent visitor—but I was getting busier and busier, hiring instructors and renting pianos and distributing fliers and posters. On September 1 the school was ready for business and by October it was filled to the rafters with jittery young pianists and chirping little ballerinas.

On my last day as tutor, the Olszewskis threw a lavish dinner party for me. It was just like the Christmas Eve party—it included the same people pretty much and it took place on the second floor. In fact, the table that was used at Christmas was set up in the hallway. Needless to say, there was enough food and drink for ten parties. It was a grand time and I think I drank a bit too much— rum and Cokes—and became slightly stinko—giving a loud stupid speech about what a joy the last six years had been, what a wonderful student and mentor Adam had been—and what a blast it was working alongside the PMP crew. When the party was over and pop was taking me home, Mrs. Olszewska gave me a large manila envelope. Inside it was one of Adam's most recent drawings of yours truly—but as I'd been six years before. Why he chose the girlish me as a subject I don't know—but there I was, wearing a pinafore and ankle socks, nervous but determined, toting my lunch pail and book-stuffed backpack. In the corner was a red Pie Man Pie logo and under that, in red ink, words from a Latin lesson.

Amor animi arbitrio sumitur, non ponitur.
We choose to start loving, but not to stop.

21

DURING THE 1970S, I KEPT IN PRETTY CLOSE touch with Adam—visiting him every so often, keeping him up to date as to how MGA was doing, regaling him with tales of the relentlessly untalented children I taught and the miserable parents I avoided—or tried to—at every turn. And eight years later, my dear Adam was the first to know that MGA had closed down—failed—returned eventually to its first life as a Chinese restaurant, overwhelmed by community indifference. I also kept in touch with Adam about my pop's slow decline—his chest pains and difficulty breathing—about my private piano students and the various lotharios who tried to get into my life—and pants. Then, in 1980, I wrote Adam a long letter to tell him that I had married an older, wealthy man—my sad Mr. M. He wanted me to reopen MGA, possibly in New Haven—all those faculty brats—but I declined, preferring instead to live off the income his construction business brought in. I became the baroness of backhoes, the countess of caterpillars—and when poor Mr. M.'s heart failed, I became the sole owner of the business since he had no family to speak of. Several years later I sold the company and retired to Florida to live among wealthy right-wing cranks and the other similarly delightful souls I found there. That was in 1991.

The next time I wrote at length—Christmas cards don't count—it was to inform Adam of my marriage to a man—Mr. P.—who was younger than Mr. M. but also had a troubled heart and didn't live terribly long—I sure know how to pick 'em. Mr. P. looked like one of Picasso's *saltimbanques*—he possessed a flat, bland tragic beauty. We traveled a great deal before he kicked the bucket—visiting the capitals of the world—which was fun. But what I thought about while visiting them were the cities Adam named after me when he drew his maps. Adam never wrote me a proper letter. Now and then he sent me a post card with a drawing on the back, but I never received any news about whether he had left his room. I often imagined that he had, but deep down I knew that he hadn't.

BETSY

IN JANUARY 1971 (MY FOURTH YEAR WITH PIE MAN Pies), I received my degree in mathematics and, that same year, was engaged to be married, became an American citizen, and was offered a job teaching algebra in New Haven. Miss T. (I called her Bea) had left by then to start her music school, so Adam was without companionship during the day, although the twelve-year-old boy next door, Alex Glowac, often visited him after school. Adam had helped me so very much with my liberal arts classes, but when I told him through his bedroom door that I had decided to study mathematics, he laughed and told me I was on my own. Still, he was my advocate, my secret champion. It was his idea that Pie Man Pies pay for my education and books and anything else I needed for school; this included an old Dodge sedan *Pan* Olszewski found and repaired.

There was, of course, a going-away party when I left; it was a small get together, subdued, not the raucous celebration they had for Bea. The Olszewskis gave me a handsome pen and pencil set, Danuta gave me a lovely scarf from Poland, and Adam, as expected, gave me (via his mother) one of his sketches, a lovely portrait of me reading a book. Before I left for home that evening, I knocked on his door and whispered, "Thank you, thank you for everything."

The day of the party was the last time I saw Adam's parents or any of the pie-making women. My husband (also a math teacher and one of Helena's original dates) and I eventually moved to Michigan, far from everything, but cozy enough to give us all the peace and quiet and privacy we could want. In truth, we became very much like Adam, hermits who rarely left our own little world. In the summer, we grew vegetables and lovely irises, swam in a nearby lake, and enjoyed picnics and cookouts; in the winter, we read books and watched movies and sat around our wood stove. We didn't keep to our rooms, of course, but we mostly kept to ourselves and we still do. We have a few friends, good friends, but we rarely socialize and we aren't churchgoers and we don't belong to clubs of any kind. That's all ok with us, but I admit that we have lost touch with *Pani* Olszewska and everyone from that time in my life; there's some sadness in that.

ALEX GLOWAC

1

TO ADAM OLSZEWSKI, OUR NEIGHBORHOOD WAS the matrix that surrounded the jewel of his house, so he took pride in knowing everything that happened in it. He knew when someone was ill, was born, died, moved. He knew who was friends with whom. He knew what adults did for a living and how youngsters did in school. He was like a spy watching life go by in the greater Peru Street area, listening to people chat as they walked up and down the walkway, listening to the gossip of his mother's Pie Man Pies employees. Listening and watching and learning. A spy and a spider. Quite often, though, the information he collected was information about himself or at least what we, his neighbors, thought of him, or, more exactly, imagined him to be like. A lot of what he heard about himself came from me and my various pals who spent our summer evenings in the little park on Peru Street, sitting around a picnic table talking about sports and girls and, with surprising frequency, the inscrutable hermit who lived just two houses away. And all within hearing distance from Adam, since voices tended to carry in that still summer night air.

From his eavesdropping, Adam knew that while we accepted him as part of the neighborhood, he was also a mystery to us, a brooding, unseen presence. He knew that we called him Adam O. or Adam Pie Man or simply Pie Man, connecting him, out of ignorance, really, to his mother's business. He also knew that some of us claimed at one time or another to have seen his face in the house's second-floor window. Actually, that was a fairly common occurrence. Adam didn't always do such a great job hiding behind his ecru curtains when he was spying on the neighborhood. Only I, however, had seen Adam *outside* the house, smoking a cigarette late at night among his mother's flowers and tomatoes, and only I had heard muffled music coming from his backyard at two or three in the morning, the screech of opera or the crash of percussion or the sad refrains of a Chopin nocturne.

A number of us, me included, had older cousins and brothers and sisters who had visited the Olszewski house once or twice, actually stepped foot in Adam's room and played games with him and ate candy and pie with him, and it was their recollections of a moonfaced kid who liked to draw and had some kind of rare disease that made up the core of what we knew about Adam. Some kids argued that Adam didn't exist and probably never had, a myth created by those same older boys and girls, while others believed that an Adam Olszewski had once lived in the gray house on Peru Street, but had died sometime after our older cousins and brothers and sisters had stopped visiting him, leaving a legacy of reclusion behind him like a ghost. Sightings of Adam in his second-floor window, these apostates said, were either delusions or fictions. In addition, there were a few guys who didn't care if Adam were real or not, content simply to tell cruel and vulgar stories about him, involving masturbation, prostitution, even incest.

Among my friends it was assumed I knew more about Adam than anyone else. After all, I lived next door to the Olszewskis and I had actually seen and heard Adam. But all I really knew about Adam was this: the Olszewskis had an adult son who lived at home and had been confined there most of his life because of what Adam's mother called a "medical condition." Mrs. Olszewska and my mother were good neighbors, but they weren't good friends. Something kept them from ever going beyond the boundaries of politeness and neighborliness. Maybe it was just Mrs. Olszewska's need for privacy when it came to Adam, maybe it was because her business didn't leave her time for visits and chitchat. To her credit, though, she never denied Adam's existence, as some mothers might have done, fearing social ridicule or some such nonsense; but then again, she never said much about him, either. She never explained his "medical condition" or discussed his daily routine or what he was like or what interested him or why he had to be confined to that house in the first place or how a boy on the verge of manhood could possibly remain cooped up in a house for so long—even with those middle-of-the-night respites I had witnessed—without going berserk. My mother sometimes met Adam's tutor at Kozak's Market, or some of the girls who worked making pies, but they didn't know anything. The door to his room, they said, was always closed.

And, of course, my mother never pried: she didn't want to appear nosy and it was, she said, really none of her business anyway.

2

ON A HUMID SATURDAY AFTERNOON IN AUGUST 1970, I was in my backyard catching football with Edmund, one of my playground pals. He was as coordinated as a marionette and no matter how he tried he couldn't throw the football in the proper way: his hands were too small to grip it fully and effectively, so it kept dropping to the ground and rolling away from him in its flip-flopping way. Frustrated and angry, Edmund finally decided to kick the ball to me, but he shanked it instead, sending it over the currant and gooseberry bushes that separated our yard from the Olszewski garden. When I went to retrieve the ball, gliding through the slight opening between the bushes, Edmund screamed that I shouldn't go in there. He continued to make a racket, then began grabbing his crotch and squeezing it with all his might. He started backing away, his face nearly the red-brown of the football. Then he turned around and ran past the stockade fence and up the walkway until he reached Peru Street. He took a left on Bolivia and headed for St. Paul's.

"You're not afraid to come and get your ball, are you?" said a voice from behind the currant bushes. It was Mrs. Olszewska in her black bathing suit (rippling with a shimmery moire pattern). She had been tying her tomato plants, now monstrous in size, to wooden stakes with strips of old nylon stockings. She was smiling and winked at me as if to assure me that she meant no harm.

"I'm not afraid," I said and walked through the bushes into the Olszewski yard.

"But your friend, he was. What a commotion! I wonder why he was so upset."

"I don't know."

"He's not very smart, is he?"

"No, he's not."

"In fact, you might say he's dumber than a post."

"Yes." I laughed.

"Is he a friend of yours?"

"I suppose so."

"But not a good friend."

"No."

Mrs. Olszewska nodded her head, pleased, I think, that I wasn't so discourteous as to defend a boy who didn't deserve defending. She dropped her nylon strips into the wicker basket at her feet and walked over to retrieve the ball that had ended up under a dwarf azalea. She bent down to pick it up and, grabbing it with both hands, tossed it in the air a few times.

"Well, don't you want to come and get it?" she asked.

I took a few steps and stood directly in front of her. She asked about my bother, Jake, who was now at Cornell, and I told her what I knew, which wasn't much. Jake and I never really got along. Then she asked about my parents and then about my grades at school.

"All *A*'s," I said, looking at my sneakers.

"I'm not surprised," she said. "Adam thinks you're the smartest boy in the neighborhood. In fact, he says you're the smartest by far. The other ones he calls barbarians. Girls, too."

"But how does he know?"

"Oh, he sees and he listens; and he's smart, too, maybe smarter than you even. What's your favorite subject?"

"Science."

"It is, is it?"

"Yes."

"Well, I'll be sure to tell Adam. Now will you do me a favor and wait here for a second? My friends and I baked pies all morning and I have an extra blueberry I'd like you to take to your mother. I think a smart scientific boy like yourself would like a homemade pie for dessert. Maybe also a jar of the currant jelly I made last year from those currants you just walked through. Wait here, ok?"

She tossed the ball and smiled when I snatched it out of the air; then she turned to go inside and after taking a step or two turned around to face me again.

"You know, never mind," she said. "Not even someone as smart as you can carry a pie, a jar of jelly and a football all at the same time. I'll come by later on and leave the pie and jelly on your porch."

That afternoon, sprawled out on Mom's chaise lounge, I thought about Adam's life, how it must be the exact opposite of my own. I was active and physical; I mowed the lawn or played baseball. He was passive; he read, stared out his window, listened to music, spied on neighbors. My life was filled with sunlight; Adam's was defined by shadows. I went to school, walked downtown, visited the library; Adam stayed home. But, that said, I had to admit I really had no idea what his life was like in and of itself. How did he spend his time? How could he live without friends? Was he miserable, embittered, troubled?

I also thought about my brother Jake. He'd been one of the older kids who had visited Adam in his room. In fact, Jake probably went there a lot more often than any kid in the neighborhood. He told me he wasn't allowed to go inside Adam's room, but had to remain outside the door in the hallway. I believed him at the time, but since I had seen Adam outside the friendly confines of his house, I reconsidered Jake's report and started thinking of it as a fiction or one of his famous exaggerations. It really didn't matter anyway because eventually Jake and Adam came to dislike each other and didn't see each other at all. I often wondered what happened between them. Did Adam ever think of Jake, who, as far as I could tell, had been his only friend on Earth? Certainly Adam must know about Jake's accomplishments, his academic and athletic successes. And I wondered: did that make him jealous? Had he ever been so honored? Or even simply noticed? I wanted to talk to Jake about his boyhood relationship with Adam, but he was such a pain in the ass now that he was a college man. He did tell me once that he and Adam used to play chess in the hallway outside Adam's room, shouting out moves through the door. Jake beat him time and time again. The last time Jake visited Adam was around Christmas a few years back. Mom said Jake came home very angry and said he didn't want to play chess with Adam ever again, which surprised her because Jake never lost at chess to anyone.

3

THAT NIGHT, I BORROWED MY DAD'S ARMY binoculars, moved my bed closer to the window that faced the Olszewski house, and waited for Adam to appear. I even kept notes:

> Clear. Stars out. A. is up. Heard music. Must be transistor. Piano, violin. Very faint & tinny. I hear A. walking around the yard. Slight clicking sound. Like an instrument of some kind. Zippo? A. doesn't use a flashlight. Able to find his way. Never bumps into anything. I see orange glow thru binocs. A little cloud. A cigarette. I faintly see A.'s face in orange light when he drags on cig. Does A. ever feel loneliness? Or is he immune by now?

I dropped off around four in the morning and slept late. Around eleven, Mom woke me up saying that Mrs. Olszewska had called and invited me to have lunch with Adam.

At five of noon, I (carrying a bouquet of black-eyed susans, which I had, under Mom's supervision, cut from her garden) walked through the opening between the bushes and found Mrs. Olszewska waiting for me on the other side. It was another hot, steamy day and she was dressed in shorts and a white t-shirt printed with the red Pie Man Pies logo. Her face was flushed and sweaty and, here and there, on her cheeks, hands, and arms, there were small explosions of flour. I gave her the flowers; she smiled as she accepted them and said that she had always admired them from a distance. Then I entered the house through the kitchen door. I was trembling but tried to conceal the fact. I don't think I did a good job of it because Mrs. Olszewska put her hand on the back of my neck and started rubbing as if to console me.

Inside, Mrs. Olszewska introduced me to her best friend, Danuta, who was also dressed in shorts and a Pie Man t-shirt and was spotted with flour as well. She was washing bowls, measuring cups, rolling pins, and wooden spoons in a large metal sink. Then I was introduced to two sisters, Anna Maria and Zosia, both with short black hair, black eyes, and olive complexions, and another young woman named Betsy, who kind of looked like Madam Curie. On large tables, protected by a blue-checkered oil cloth, were dozens of pies: all ready for delivery. Mrs. Olszewska told me that her pie business was in a relatively quiet period. People were on vacation and didn't buy pies, so orders were down. But in a week or two, when the summer was over, people would start craving pies again, and she and the girls would get back to their busy schedule. Mrs. Olszewska and I then walked to the den where she introduced me to Wanda Kozak, who was on her lunch break. She was slouched on a blue sofa watching a soap opera, her chin touching her chest, her feet crossed at the ankles. I thought she was very pretty, but in an odd and inexplicable way. She had the look of someone who was on the verge of going to sleep. I went to shake her hand, but she gave me a quick mechanical wave and I stopped in my tracks.

We continued through the downstairs rooms. I noticed that, except for the kitchen, the house was extremely dark; the outdoor light was muted and even a sunny day like the one I had just come from had a gloomy, rainy-day look to it. When we reached the stairwell, Mrs. Olszewska pointed to the top and told me to go up and take a right when I ran out of steps. She mussed my hair and returned to the kitchen, saying she would return in a while with lunch and a piece of pie. Adam, she added, had already eaten. Then she showed me the secret knock: one, two, three, four. Beethoven's Fifth. When I reached the top of the stairs, I continued to my right, tiptoeing as I went, like a spy in a cartoon. I knocked the secret knock, but heard nothing. Then I heard a voice, a man's voice, deep and resonant. It sounded as though he were talking an inch or so from the wood of the door. It seemed for a second that the door was doing the talking.

"So you've been spying on me," the voice said.

"Me?"

"Sure, last night. You were spying on me with your binoculars, taking notes, too, I think."

"I was just curious."

"Good, good," the voice said. "It's good you have curiosity. It's what killed the cat, but you're not a cat, are you?"

Adam spoke with a precision and a gentleness I had never heard before in a human voice. Every word he uttered seemed taken from a dreamy, slow song.

"So," he continued, "is your curiosity of a scientific or literary bent? I mean, are you interested in me *per se* or in me as a member of *Homo reclusus*. You know, Boswell or Darwin. If it's Darwin, and I think it is, then I must be one of his finches and one day I'll tell you about the origin of my species."

Just then, Mrs. Olszewska appeared at the top of the stairs carrying a tray that held a sandwich, a glass of ginger ale, and a generous slab of cherry pie. It was a ham-and-cheese sandwich with lettuce, a garden tomato, and mayo on rye, my absolute favorite. As I ate, Adam talked.

"To answer the question you have asked yourself but might be too polite to repeat, I have to say, Mr. Darwin, that, no, I don't feel pangs of loneliness. The fact is, I'm not alone that often. I have my parents and there's Danuta and the others; but, yes, I know what you mean. Do I feel left out? Do I feel that life has passed me by? In all honesty, no. It's not that I dislike people, I just don't need them. As for you, well, I was also curious about you, maybe in the same way you were curious about me. You're not like the other kids in the neighborhood. You're smart and inquisitive and you're certainly not like your brother Jake. As far as I can tell, you have good manners and a vivid imagination and you don't think so highly of yourself."

"Jake thinks he's a real big shot," I said.

Adam laughed. "Yes, he does."

4

IN TIME I BECAME A REGULAR VISITOR TO THE Olszewski house. When I dropped by after school during the week, I was usually scooted upstairs by Mrs. Olszewska or Danuta, or even one of the Italian sisters, who were too busy, to my regret, to pay me any mind (when they did, when they fussed over me, I have to say it did my little male ego a world of good). From September to Christmas of that year, Mrs. Olszewska's kitchen was utter chaos. I thought the voices of women in the kitchen, the clumping of footsteps, the music on the radio (the sisters liked their rock 'n roll), the clatter, creak, clunk, thump and bang of preparation and baking would be nerve-racking for Adam; but he insisted he didn't mind any of it. He didn't need absolute silence to read his books or draw his pictures or keep tabs on the neighborhood. What's more, he said, *it* liked it better this way, noisy and bustling, *it* being the house. Apparently *it* thought it was Christmas Eve every day.

It took me a while to understand the extent of Adam's house fixation. I assumed it was the outside world he was afraid of and that was that. I didn't know about the house, and when he told me about his connection to it, I found it difficult to believe. Here was a young man of twenty, an intelligent, sociable, otherwise rational man who actually believed the house he lived in was alive. It protected him, nurtured him, but it was more than that. The house *was* him. Even I, a kid of twelve, knew that wasn't normal. Or sane. And if I thought about it too much, it was also kind of scary. One day I told him how weird it was for him to have such beliefs. No reply. But when I said I found it a little scary, he became very apologetic.

"Don't take it to heart," he said. "It's not that important to me anymore. It's mostly just theoretical now."

One more thing: He had only recently left his room. Apparently, it had been a pretty big step for him. After more than a decade of self-confinement, he had shuffled out of his room, walked downstairs, stepped out the kitchen door (the very doorway, he said, that refused to allow him outside so many years ago), and sat on the back porch smoking cigarettes and listening to music on a transistor radio. The thing was, no one ever saw him do it. Except me during my post-midnight surveillances. Even so, I couldn't tell what he looked like, couldn't describe him in any detail. All I knew was that he wasn't a monster. He had, from what I could see in the orange cigarette glow, an ordinary enough face. No hideous deviations from the norm. My pals, who swore they had seen his face in his bedroom window, said he looked like a vampire, but no one took them seriously. No doubt Adam was paler than pale, having avoided full contact with the sun for all those years, but the rest of it, the fangs and widow's peak and that nonsense was just that, nonsense.

"You're the only one who knows about my midnight excursions into the back yard," he said one day. "If you want to remain friends, you have to swear you won't tell anyone. Not my parents. Not your parents. Not anyone."

"But I've already told my friends," I replied.

"Oh, I know that. I meant not tell anyone with a brain."

After a while Adam started calling me "little brother," and, though I'd been a little brother all my life, it was to Jake, who never paid much attention to me and whom I never particularly liked that much anyway. I was such a frequent visitor to 7 Peru Street that my Mom thought I might be making a pest out of myself, but Mrs. Olszewska told her I could come over as often as I liked. She said Adam really enjoyed my company. Since his tutor had left to start her own business (and was not replaced on purpose) he didn't have anyone to talk to. He said I reminded him of himself in many ways. But most of all, he said, I made him laugh.

To be honest, I enjoyed having two families. My life became more complicated, but undeniably richer and more interesting. I loved my parents and I also loved being with Adam and his family. I was a very lucky boy indeed. At Halloween, Mrs. Olszewska gave me all the candy the children had left at her door for Adam and at Christmas I exchanged presents in two houses. During the school week, I often came by for dinner, after which Adam helped me with my homework, mostly English and history assignments. He had little interest in math and science, which I liked best. For help with those subjects I went to Mr. Olszewski. He was a quiet and reserved man and while he never went to college, he was intelligent, even brilliant. A self-taught man.

He and I liked to talk about anything that had to do with chemistry and physics and engineering and mechanics. One time we were in the hallway, speculating on what the future would be like: advanced robotics, we decided, plus more leisure time and larger thought capacity that translated into more selfless and noble behavior. Adam laughed from behind the door. He believed that in the future people would be more isolated. A nation of hermits, he said.

Of course, my neighborhood friends teased me about my visits to the Olszewski house, but my position as *the* expert on Adam was now inviolate and I knew something none of them knew. That *they* were never truly alone, that Adam was always watching and listening to them. That their silly theories of love and romance and their crass jokes and nasty fictions didn't go unheard.

Eventually, I talked about and defended Adam so often that my friends no longer thought he was mysterious or evil. They no longer made crude jokes about him, afraid to hurt my feelings and insult someone who had become so close to me. Maybe they were also afraid that Adam might exact revenge on them, murder them in the night. But maybe, I think, Adam had simply became one of them, one of us. Just another someone in the neighborhood.

5

EARLY IN DECEMBER I WENT UP TO THE SECOND-floor hallway and was ready to sit in my designated folding chair when I noticed there was a small Bell & Howell 8mm projector on the seat pointed toward the end of the hallway where a screen had been set up.

"It's all ready to go," Adam said from behind the door. "Just turn on the projector."

I did. The machine sputtered and, after a quick jerk, beamed an image of the Olszewski kitchen, minus a few stoves and tables. Then a young Adam came into view holding his father's hand. His face was large and round, a moon face, just as Jake had once described it.

"That's me, of course," Adam said over the rattle of the projector. "My father is going to pick me up and carry me outside. But, as you can see, the house refuses to give me up. That's Dr. Cohen. You know him. He's your doctor, too. Notice the blood pouring out of my nose, notice how I'm shaking like mad and gasping for air. That day, my seventh birthday, was the first day of my reclusion and seclusion. Since then I haven't been outside the house's domain, which now includes, as you have observed and only you know, my backyard. I understand that the movie's hard to look at, and I don't want to scare you, but if you're a true scientific investigator, a true Darwin, you shouldn't be upset because this little film shows you how and when I became a hermit. However, what it doesn't explain is why. The why has to do with me becoming this house and this house becoming me. But, you see, Dr. Cohen and his colleagues weren't interested in that kind of thinking. That was, they said, a *result* rather than an *explanation* of my condition. They said a boy doesn't become his house and vice versa. They were looking for underlying reasons; being a Darwin yourself, you probably think along similar lines. Am I right?"

Not quite understanding all of what Adam meant, I didn't say anything.

"Well, then, enough of that," Adam said. "You can turn off the projector now."

6

NEAR CHRISTMAS I VISITED ADAM, AS USUAL, scampering through the kitchen as I always did, leaping up the stairway two steps at a time and finding my chair where it always was, just to the right of his door. On this day, however, Mrs. Olszewska stopped me before I left the kitchen.

"I have something for you," she said. "Come with me."

We walked into the parlor and sat on the sofa.

"I'm sure you know how much Adam enjoys drawing. He's very good at it and, as he says, it helps him pass the time. Now and again he'll give me what he's drawn and I'll put it into a portfolio and keep it safe. On file. You know, like a library. I have everything he's drawn from the time he was a toddler. Each portfolio, you see, represents one year. So I have twenty volumes. Can you imagine? He draws everything, but mostly he draws what he sees in his room or in the neighborhood. Mrs. Wrobel he's drawn dozens of times, you know, trimming her hedges, picking rhubarb for strawberry rhubarb pie, sitting in her chaise under the big oak tree. There's even a few of Angela Wrobel before she left for California, but that was when he was a small boy. And yes, dear Alex, he's done dozens of pictures of you and your family and last week he asked me to go back over the years and pick out a few of them. The last year or so the pictures have all been of you, but I found plenty of early ones of your dad and mom and brother. There's even one of you when your mother brought you home the day after you were born."

She reached behind the sofa and pulled out a couple dozen sheets of fancy paper and placed them on the coffee table. They were drawings done in pencil or pen or charcoal as well as the occasional watercolor. She had put the sheets in roughly chronological order so the first one was of me being held by my Mom standing in the backyard next to Mrs. Olszewska. My Mom is showing me off to the neighborhood for the first time. The angle is from above, Adam looking down from his bedroom window. There were quite a few other drawings: Jake playing chess; my Mom hanging clothes and harvesting tomatoes from her garden (she and Mrs. Olszewska had a friendly competition as to who could grow the biggest Big Boys); my Dad, a bartender at Charlie's Grille, dressed up in his white shirt and red bow tie (in pencil but the bow tie is done in red crayon), ready to go to work.

That evening, I showed the drawings to my mother who, upon seeing herself in her garden cradling her infant Alex, began to tear up. Dad, who usually joked at sentimental moments, didn't say a word and then only added that Adam might be a strange young man, but he had a good heart. Jake was still at school, but when he came home for the holiday break he refused to see the portrait Adam had made of him so many years before and warned that my friendship with Adam would not end well. In January, he sent me a letter from Cornell:

> Mom says you and Adam are still friends despite my warning. That's not good. Adam is one weird hombre. Mom says you don't think he's a freak, but, little man, he is, he really is. Listen to your big brother. Don't be bamboozled. Avoid him. That's what I did.

When I began high school, I found new friends and, in my sophomore year, had a romantic fling with a girl name Denise from the other side of town, so I spent less and less time with Adam. But, unlike Jake, I continued to like and respect him and still enjoyed his company and that of his parents. Adam understood my need for friends my own age and never resented my absences.

Jake, now working at a brokerage firm in Boston, said he was delighted that my friendship with Adam was waning, but, as always, he missed the point. Our friendship wasn't waning at all. It was as strong as it ever was. I just needed to experience things on my own. I went with my friends to the library, went on dates, went to the movies, played sports. I did all the things I was supposed to do, all the things, now that I think about it, that Adam wouldn't or couldn't do. And Adam didn't mind one bit, so long as I came by every now and then. Which I did. Adam was not only my friend and substitute big brother, he was my teacher. I learned from him. His knowledge of history and art and music and literature was encyclopedic. For me, school centered on the sciences and math, all honors level, a demanding and exhausting grind. Fulfilling, certainly, but not exactly joyful. Adam filled in the gaps in my education. He suggested what books I should read, what paintings to look at, what music to listen to. And, I must admit, I always followed his suggestions to the letter, and was rarely, if ever, disappointed. Adam was even knowledgeable about sports. He bowled me over one day when he told me he enjoyed watching baseball games on TV. Did he root for a specific team? No, he said he was an objective observer, a Darwin, like me, appreciating the nuances of the game. He didn't care which team won. It was the game that mattered and he remembered every game he ever watched and could recount every one of them inning by inning.

7

WHEN I WAS A STUDENT AT SILVERTON HIGH, there was a great commotion in the neighborhood. Mrs. Wrobel had a heart attack and her daughter, the famed beauty Angela, had come home from California to take care of her. I remember the first time I saw her, sunbathing in her back yard. She was as beautiful as people said, as beautiful as a movie star, which she apparently had tried to become when she took off for Hollywood (I was three or so at the time). I tried to, in my blunt and awkward fourteen-year-old way, strike up a conversation with her, but she wasn't very communicative and seemed to think I was a pest, which I was. She wasn't one of those young women who think adolescent boys are cute beyond imagining. In fact, I don't think she liked kids at all.

To me, what was most interesting about Angela was Adam's interest in her. Angela moved in with her mother and took care of her. She got a few part-time jobs as a waitress, but a couple years later, in the spring of 1973, my dad got her a job at Charlie's, full-time with benefits. Adam said after Mrs. Wrobel died, he often chatted with Angela late at night, whispering through the cucumber vines while Angela whispered through the walkway fence. She'd come home from the restaurant (my dad drove her to and from work) just when Adam would be beginning his nocturnal sojourns. On these occasions, he said, he mostly listened. Angela talked about her mom, her job, the jerks she served (I knew about those guys from my dad), that sort of thing. I asked him once if he thought Angela was beautiful, and he laughed and said only someone with a crush on her would ask that question. I admitted I was hopelessly in love with her. Well, he said, so was he. He had drawn her dozens of times.

8

ONE WEEKEND NIGHT IN SEPTEMBER DURING MY junior year at high school, I came home very late from a party. I was a little drunk, but was in full control of my faculties. At least I thought I was. Trying not to wake up my parents, I coasted the last hundred feet of the driveway and tiptoed up the back stairs. When I reached for the doorknob to let myself in the house, I heard tinny, muted music from beyond the currant bushes. It was as if an orchestra were playing inside a soup can. It was Adam.

I decided to sneak up on him, maybe even get a glimpse of him (maybe of Angela, too, but I could see she wasn't there). In all the time we'd been friends I'd never visited him late at night when he was outside his room, when he was vulnerable, so to speak, open to scrutiny like everyone else in the world. There were those first few times when I had spied on him, but that was all; I guess I kind of respected his privacy all those years. Anyway, he never invited me to visit him in his yard and, in fact, he rarely talked about his late-night escapades and turned quiet when I brought them up. I think it was because he was still very unsure of himself, still didn't feel comfortable being outside his room. Anyway, I had no chance at all of really sneaking up on him. He knew where I was all along, as if he had night vision.

"Looking for something?" he asked, sitting on the steps that led to the kitchen.

"I was just trying to spy on you," I said, sitting on the same steps a few feet away, or so I thought, since it was pretty dark. "You're the only friend I have whose face I've never seen."

"Nothing much to look at, I'm afraid. I'm not Joseph Merrick, you know."

Still joking around, I asked him to light his cigarette lighter and place it close to his face. There was no reply. I reached out to touch him, but touched nothing but the late summer air. I heard the screen door open and close and knew that Adam was back inside, within the boundaries of his truest and safest dominion.

9

WHEN I WENT OFF TO CAL TECH IN 1976, ADAM and I wrote to each other regularly. He followed my academic career with great interest and, in his letters (rare) and post cards (weekly), urged me on. He also reported on the neighborhood and took great pleasure in satirizing my old friends in hilarious mock-Socratic dialogues. Adam also wrote about my mother's tomatoes and how they rivaled his mother's in plumpness and redness; and he sent me newspaper accounts when Charlie's Grille burned to the ground, forcing my father to find a job at another establishment, O'Malley's, for which, Adam wrote, he wore a green bow tie instead of a red one. He wrote about his parents and chronicled births and deaths, new neighbors, and the continued success of Pie Man Pies. At the end of his brief reports, he usually added a line or two about himself: his reading, his artwork, his wanting to take up poetry again but then deciding against it. But these were only flashes of information and no matter how I, in my return letters, asked him to expound on them, he never did.

ANGELA WROBEL

1

I LEFT HOME WHEN I WAS EIGHTEEN AND returned when I was twenty-eight. I didn't leave for Hollywood. I just left. Unlike my mom, I had no interest at all in the movies and I wasn't some starry-eyed little girl with a head full of stupid dreams. All I wanted to do was leave home, be my own person, and have some fun. I returned because my mom had suffered a heart attack and needed me. She had no one else to take care of her. Agnes Olszewska had watched over her until I arrived and was a true friend throughout the whole ordeal.

I hadn't been the best daughter in the world, so this was a chance for me to show my stuff. I'd left everything I had in California, although that wasn't a hell of a lot. I was out of work at the time and living with a heroin addict named Baker, an actor who never acted, a writer who never wrote, an artist who never painted. We lived in a sad little flat not far from Hollywood itself. In a way I was almost glad my mom had had her heart attack. It was an excuse for me to leave LA for good.

According to Agnes, my mom collapsed on Peru Street right in front of our house. It was early in the morning, a lovely, early May morning, and she was on her way to the courthouse downtown where she worked as a secretary. Anna Maria, one of the Pie Man girls, saw the whole thing. She created such a racket that Agnes herself came out to see what was the matter. By the time she went inside again to call for an ambulance, one had already arrived.

Later, I became friendly with Anna Maria. Actually, she treated me like some kind of goddess. It was because I'd lived in LA. When I saw her on Peru Street one time and thanked her again for helping my mom, she asked me a hundred questions about California. Soon, she started wearing her hair the way I did and wore the same kinds of jewelry and clothes, too. I had to laugh. My hair was a disaster. My so-called jewels were the cheapest of trinkets. My clothes were hippyish rags.

My mom stayed in the hospital for two days. By the time I arrived she was already home, waiting for me, sitting up in bed. Agnes was at her side feeding her broth and promising her pie if she finished it all. It was the first time I'd seen my mom in ten years. We took one look at each other and started bawling. Even Agnes joined in. I felt I was being given a second chance. No more heroin addicts. No more LA bullshit. In my suitcase were the remnants of my pathetic wardrobe and a few mementos, all I owned in the world. The airplane ticket had depleted my savings and my personal fortune amounted to the eight bucks and change I had in my purse. Agnes said I looked thin, much thinner than she remembered, and promised to remedy that. I laughed, imagining a conveyor belt carrying pies from her house to ours.

I moved into the upstairs rooms, which we had often rented out, but were now empty. That night, our first together, I apologized for having been such a terrible daughter, a real snot and know-it-all. And so full of myself! But she said I was being too self-critical. What was important was that I had returned home when I was needed.

Those first few weeks with my mom were absolutely wonderful. For once, we were relaxed in each other's company. Conversation flowed effortlessly. I made dinner, cleaned the house, cut the lawn, trimmed the privet hedge, and waited on my mom, the perfect patient. She read mysteries, something new for her. She had outgrown her movie fan magazines. Many of them had vanished anyway, gone out of business, I suppose. And neither of us could imagine anyone ever reading those foolish newspapers for sale in supermarket checkout aisles. I was surprised to learn that my mom hadn't been to a movie theater in years. I suggested that we go, maybe when it got hot, if only to take advantage of the air conditioning. But she balked. She saw no reason to see films that might disturb or even disgust her. Anyway, she said she'd rather watch old movies on TV.

After a few weeks my mom was feeling much better. She was well enough to go back to work, part time at first, then according to her normal schedule. I'd already begun looking for work. Agnes said she would hire me and I was grateful for the offer, but since I wasn't much of a cook, I could only be a liability in her kitchen. One time Agnes asked me what kinds of jobs I had had in California, half expecting me to say *extra* or even *actress*. And when I said *waitress*, she looked a little surprised. Then, rebounding a bit, she said she'd ask Mrs. Glowac to talk to her bartender husband and find out if there was something for me at Charlie's Grille. In the meanwhile I had landed a couple part-time jobs. One was at Vitolini's, an Italian restaurant that Agnes and Mr. O. frequented. I worked the slow days, Tuesday and Wednesday, so I didn't make much. I also waitressed Friday night at the Silverton Diner to help with the weekend rush. I sold quite a few Pie Man pies there. For the first time I understood how much people liked them.

When I wasn't working, I was looking for real work. Full-time work. I went on interviews in the morning and, if I had nothing else to do, spent my afternoons sunbathing even though it was still May and not as warm as I would have liked. Not California warm anyway. The yard was only a patch of lawn with an ever-spreading plot of rhubarb my father had planted the year I was born. The yard got unobstructed sun all afternoon. Across the walkway I could see the Pie Man ladies in the kitchen window at 7 Peru Street. I wondered how Agnes managed to keep the noise down. In my waitressing experience, kitchens were always ear-piercingly loud places. Once in a while I spoke with Agnes or Danuta when they were on break. Sometimes they brought out a piece of pie for me.

When I was sunbathing I wore the skimpiest of bikinis. But I didn't care. No one could see me. I was completely alone, at least until three o'clock when the neighborhood kids were let out of school. Most of them, boys, of course, stood at the top of the walkway steps on Peru Street and craned their neck so they could see me over our hedge. But some of the older boys were bolder. Little Alex Glowac was the boldest of them all, a smooth talker, but I had no time for him and scooted him away, which probably hurt his feelings, but I just wasn't in the mood for adolescent chatter.

One day, on a whim, I loosened my bikini top and went completely uncovered. I applied my usual mixture of baby oil and iodine to my skin, a recipe for fast tanning I'd learned from Agnes herself. Then it hit me: I'd been so preoccupied with being bothered by Alex and his little buddies that I had completely forgotten about Adam. The only direct view into my backyard was from Adam's bedroom window. I covered myself in two seconds flat.

To be honest, I hadn't really thought about Adam at all. I'd been his favorite babysitter when he was a little cutie and had a crush on me. But that was such a long time ago. I started wondering what kind of young man he'd become locked up inside that house for all those years. Agnes hadn't mentioned him, and I didn't know if that was a good thing or a bad thing. She hadn't mentioned her husband, either. Maybe Adam had become even more of a hermit, more withdrawn, more afraid of the outside world. Or maybe he'd become completely normal. Whenever I was in the backyard, I would glance up at Adam's window. The curtain was always drawn, the shade always pulled down. The next time I spoke with Agnes, I asked her how Adam was doing and whether he remembered me.

"Oh, he's doing just fine," she said. "And he remembers you all right. He was always very fond of you. He still is."

2

I REMEMBERED ADAM'S DRAWINGS, PICTURES OF me and my mom, and then these goofy maps of imagined lands with names based on my name. He was such a talented little boy, a prodigy, I guess. He had a real crush on me and loved it when I came over to babysit. He'd show me his drawings and sometimes I'd sit for him, his model, like he was a grown-up artist and we were in Paris or something. I guess he was really a weird little kid, but he was also so sweet and so grown up. I never had any trouble with him. I'd tell Agnes and Mr. O. when they came home from the movies or wherever they went that they didn't even have to call me over: Adam could babysit himself.

When I was in high school, I didn't sit with Adam very much if at all. I was popular and had an active social life. I was always going out somewhere, to the movies or a dance or party or somewhere. My mother took my place and, even though Adam had a crush on me, the change didn't matter one bit to him. He kind of had a crush on my mom, too. He loved movies almost as much as she did and they'd spend the evening talking about this movie or that, this movie star or that. But then something odd happened. When I was his babysitter, Adam wouldn't go outside, but was free to go anywhere in the house. All that changed. My mom came home one night and said that Adam had locked himself in his room and refused to go outside it. After that when they talked about movies they did so through his bedroom door. When they watched movies together he watched on the TV in his room and she watched on a portable in the hallway. That Adam, she said, is some strange kid.

3

AFTER I'D BEEN BACK A FEW WEEKS I STARTED imagining what Adam might look like, tall and thin and pale, with a soft resonant voice, a thin lean-shaven face that had long ago lost its babyfat and roundness. I imagined that he had grown up to be quite a handsome young man, with particularly attractive black eyes, very mysterious and very seductive.

4

JOBS WERE SCARCE THAT SUMMER AND I SPENT almost all of my free time in my yard. I was as dark as Agnes. I no longer sunbathed in the seminude. In part because I knew for certain that Adam was watching me, in part because it was already June and school was out and the neighborhood was crawling with kids, young Alex, who was, I learned, Adam's pal and "little brother," among them. The kids hung out in the playground on Peru Street sitting around a picnic table talking about who knows what. They stayed there until midnight, sometimes later.

One night in early July, when I was on the verge of sleep, I turned off my end-table lamp, as I did every night, but found it difficult to sleep. My mind was racing, zooming like crazy. I was worried about everything: money, getting a job, my mom's health. I noticed that I had, earlier that day when I was cleaning my room, left the curtain open and the shade up. Through the open window I saw the darkness of the Olszewski house, then a dim bluish glow in what I guessed was the parlor window, probably a residue of TV light from the den. Adam's window was completely dark, just as mine would have been to him. Pitch blackness, I thought, must be a voyeur's best friend and worst enemy: he could find safety in it, but couldn't see into it. Why I assumed Adam was a voyeur I couldn't say, although it certainly made sense that someone would have peeping Tom tendencies after staying in his room for twenty years.

I thought about reading myself to sleep, but I didn't want to turn on the end-table lamp. Too bright. Instead, I got up and went into the bathroom. There I turned on the fluorescent light and closed the door except for a slight crack. My bedroom now had a soft bluish-green glow to it, like a motel swimming pool. Back in bed, I took off my nightgown and underwear and kicked away the top sheets. Almost immediately I felt the weight of Adam's eyes on my body. I stared at the bluish-green ceiling and thought about him, imagining him with a velvety soft voice and black eyes and skin as white as china. I was about to touch myself but thought better of it. No hands. Hands were clumsy inert things. Claws, paws, talons, tentacles. Looking was better than touching; it exposed secrets and then shared them: it was the sex of angels. I have to say, it was a kick being looked at, made love to from far away. From then on I slept without sheets or blankets; curtains remained open, shade up. I had sex with Adam every night after that, intact and untouched.

5

WHEN I LEFT FOR CALIFORNIA IN 1961, I DIDN'T leave alone. I was accompanied by a high school friend called Chi Chi. He was very attentive to me, but then so was every other boy in school. But Chi Chi not only promised to be my rescuing knight, he actually was. He won my respect, and, for a time at least, my heart. He bought an old Plymouth for thirty bucks, got his driver's license, and earned travel money loading trucks after school. The Plymouth ran, but only barely, unable to go more than forty miles per hour. That was enough for me. It meant that for every hour that passed, I would be forty miles farther away from Silverton.

Chi Chi and I left on a sunny day in 1961. The Plymouth was really a beat-up piece of shit. There was a hole in the floor behind the passenger seat so we had to be careful about accidentally stepping into (or being sucked into) the hole and ending up splattered all over the road. We were overjoyed that the car made it to New York City. We stopped in one of those automat places where you get food in glass compartments. I had a tuna fish sandwich that tasted like cat food spread between two layers of dust. It was too expensive to stay for very long, so we moved on. We weren't headed for Hollywood. That's just what I told my mom to make her happy. She was so movie-crazy back then, following the lives of the stars and all. How many women back then knew that kind of stuff? Or even cared about it?

No, we weren't headed for Hollywood. We were just headed west.

We drove through Ohio and Indiana and then the car broke down outside of Terre Haute. It cost us fifty dollars to get the thing running again, which left us severely short of cash. We stayed in St. Louis for a few months with Chi Chi's aunt and uncle. He knew a mechanic who somehow managed to hammer the Plymouth back into decent shape. I made a few extra bucks waiting tables at a little Italian place that specialized in Chicago-style pizza, which Chi Chi and I didn't like very much. Outside of the New Haven area, he said, no one knew how to make pizza. He called it *abeetz*. After a while we were off again. Kansas City, Dodge City (Chi Chi, who loved Westerns, wanted to see it, but it wasn't much to see), then into Denver. We had planned on crossing the Rockies, but Chi Chi realized he wasn't very fond of huge mountains and severe heights so we headed south into New Mexico and Arizona. We saw the big meteor hole, the petrified forest, the Grand Canyon, and Tombstone, of course, and the OK Corral, and then Nogales. We crossed the desert and entered California from the south, following the Santa Fe railroad line. It was 120 degrees. One morning I had a cup of hot coffee at a little cafe in the middle of nowhere and it almost knocked me out. Honey, the waitress said, if you ain't used to the desert you shouldn't be drinkin' no hot coffee.

When we got into LA, we found a dumpy little room near the college. I got a job waitressing and Chi Chi found a part-time job loading trucks. We lived there for five years. Then I got involved with a bunch of beats. Maybe hippies. Maybe both. They wrote poetry, I think. I didn't care one way or the other. I mostly liked them because of the pot. Oh yes, I fell deeply in love with weed, couldn't get enough of it, couldn't get in or out of bed without it. It was a scene Chi Chi didn't like at all and eventually he split. He came back east, was arrested for breaking and entering, and ended up in jail. Isn't it funny how things happen?

Then I lived in Eugene, Oregon, for a time and then San Francisco, where *everyone* was smoking dope. Then I ended up back in LA, but I was already sick of the place, sick of the people, everyone so pushy, everyone looking out for only themselves. Friendship was only a truce among rivals, no one cared about anyone else. If someone did something to forward his or her career, people were nice and polite and had great things to say, but inside they were seething with jealousy. It was pretty sick, really. The weather was pleasant all right, but the place was choking on all the failures it created. There were only so many drug store discoveries to be made. And you know what? Underneath all the glamour and crap it was really just an ordinary, cheesy little town. The movie stars and producers and all the successful people might have lived there, but no one saw them. Success made the successful invisible, at least to people like me. I took a few college courses, but my heart wasn't in it and I dropped out. I was never a very good student anyway, the only business I knew was the restaurant business and what could school teach me about that?

During my last few years there I worked at a fancy restaurant near Beverly Hills and made excellent tips. To get the job I had to interview with the owner, Mr. Edgar, a fat, creepy man in his fifties who liked his waitresses smart, friendly, good looking, and blonde. I did some investigating on my own and found out that no one liked him at all. None of the cooks or waiters or bartenders or busboys, but, lucky for everyone, he never spent much time at the restaurant. He was always at this race track, Hollywood Park. He liked me (men like him always do) and hired me then and there. He liked that I was a New Englander, although he was disappointed when I said I'd never been to Narragansett or Yonkers.

At Mr. Edgar's, I served all sorts of big shots, mostly pigs. If it weren't for a few old gents, I wouldn't have worked there at all, no matter how good the money. The old guys were happy just to make conversation. They talked about the weather or politics or about the good old days when men had manners. They thought enough of me to ask my opinion and they found me interesting enough to ask about my life, no risqué remarks, no boorishness, just a pleasant exchange, the simple, respectful curiosity one person has for another. And the money *was* good, very good. I moved into a nice apartment, ditched my weed-smoking friends, and started to make a life for myself. I started going out with one of the chefs in the kitchen, not a poet or artist, just a regular guy from New Mexico who didn't smoke dope and thought a desert filled with nothing was more beautiful than anywhere filled with everything. Unfortunately, the business wasn't run that well. All the restaurant's profits either went up Mr. Edgar's nose or were lost at the track. After a while I was out of work again, except this time I had this apartment I could no longer afford and a car that I had to sell to pay off the bank loan. I had to sell my nice new clothes. The chef moved back to New Mexico and I moved in with Baker, the heroin addict. I couldn't get any lower, it seemed, when I got a call from Agnes about my mom's heart attack. I got my affairs in order and took what little money I had out of the bank. Then I came home.

6

TWO YEARS AFTER MY MOM'S FIRST HEART attack, she had a second, which turned out to be the last thing she ever did on earth. Adam, I figured out, had witnessed both attacks. The first time, Adam was the one who called for an ambulance just as Anna Maria began screaming hysterically, alerting the neighbors. The second time, at least according to Agnes, Adam had been drawing goldfinches or something and had called the ambulance when he saw my mom was in trouble.

She had been walking up Peru Street on her way home from work, but instead of going inside the house, she went to get a piece of newspaper lodged in the privet hedge. Adam had been drawing away. When he saw my mother he flipped the page in his notebook or artist's pad or whatever it was and, again this is according to Agnes, he started to draw her, quick dashes in pencil of my mom reaching across the hedge for the yellowed piece of newspaper. That's when she howled in pain and fell into the hedge. Adam probably dropped his pad and pencil, went to make the phone call in his parents' bedroom (Agnes said he didn't have one in his room or didn't want one, I don't remember which) and dialed the operator who made the necessary connections. In a matter of a few minutes an ambulance was on its way, but it arrived too late. I came home about twenty minutes later, returning from a job interview I should never have gone on. Some kind of stupid job selling door to door. That night, Agnes called and offered her condolences and explained Adam's role in all this. She said Adam was very distraught, having been witness to my mom's last minutes on earth. She said Adam wanted to give me drawings he had made of my mom over the years. I said yes, yes, that would be wonderful, if there was anything I wanted at that moment it was a portrait of my mom, some likeness I could hold close to my heart and take with me everywhere. She said he also had some drawings of me, but these, I said as politely as I could, I would have to refuse.

That night, I couldn't sleep. I went outside and sat at the edge of my chaise smoking cigarettes. I heard some rustling in the Olszewski yard beyond the fence with cucumber vines hanging from it. I thought it might be Adam and in a kind of stage whisper I called out his name. Adam? Adam? But no one answered. I had assumed that Adam never left his room, so I wasn't the least bit disappointed that he wasn't outside to answer me. But then, I thought, he had to leave his room to make the emergency phone call, so he wasn't exactly a prisoner in his cell: he could move around the house, maybe even go outside on pleasant summer nights.

I saw or thought I saw the orange glow of a lit cigarette, and I called out again. Adam? Adam? He might have been outside watching me, but it was clear he wasn't going to answer me. So I thanked him for the drawings of my mom, which Agnes had dropped off earlier in the evening. I had glanced through them and saw how very good they were and what a superb artist Adam really was. The drawings captured something special about my mom, I don't know what, maybe her generosity, her patience, her capacity for love. He also sneaked in a portrait of me. It wasn't of me naked in my bed, it was of me, full dressed in my best interview clothes, sitting in my chaise lounge looking through the want ads in the daily paper.

I called out his name again, but this time I didn't whisper. I got off the chaise and walked up to the fence that divided our backyard from the walkway, and I asked him point blank and in a normal volume if my mom had suffered during her last few minutes. There was a long silence; then I heard Adam's voice, a deep, resonant baritone, just like I imagined; it was as if the night had created the voice, as if the night was speaking: "No, as far as I could tell, she didn't."

Then I heard a screen door close.

7

A FEW DAYS AFTER MY MOM DIED, MR. GLOWAC called me to say that a waitress at Charlie's Grille had moved out of town, to LA of all places, and that I should call and schedule an interview. I expected Charlie to be another Mr. Edgar, another drooly creep, but I was pleasantly surprised when he turned out to be more like one of the courteous old gents I knew in California. He was in his seventies, soft-spoken, gentle. He was very sorry about my mom, and said he saw in me someone who was no stranger to hardship, but who was optimistic and cheerful nonetheless. He hired me the next day and was thoughtful enough to give me an extra week to mourn my mom's passing.

I worked until two in the morning most nights, my kind of schedule, and when I got home, I leaned on the walkway fence chatting and sharing a smoke with Adam, but I never was able to see him. He was too wily for that. He always sat on the back steps, concealed by darkness. Our chats weren't very long or even that interesting, not because of Adam, who was his usual intelligent self, but because of me, who blabbed on and on about the dumbest things, the result, no doubt, of being overtired. Some nights I was too pooped to talk, and I just listened to him, nodding my head yes to keep myself from nodding off. A lot of the time, Adam talked about my mom and her love for the movies. He knew all the actors in all the movies, who directed what, who was editor and art director, all that stuff. My mom was just interested in the movie stars, what foods they liked, how they were discovered, and so on.

It seemed to me that Adam and I were becoming friends, post-midnight pals. I was, it's true, disappointed that Adam didn't come to the funeral even though I knew perfectly well there was no way he'd ever go out in public. For a few weeks straight we talked almost every night, a beat lonely waitress and a charming, faceless hermit. When the weather turned stormy, I suggested that Adam call me and we continue our chats over the phone, but he didn't want to do that. I knew he didn't have a phone in his room. What I didn't know was that he hated talking on phones period. When he'd called the ambulance after my mom suffered her heart attacks, he had used the phone in his parents' bedroom, which, for him, was a big deal. I assumed he meant he had risked being seen by the Pie Man girls. But he had actually risked being seen *by his parents*. What? I asked, not believing what I was hearing. Wouldn't it be ok, I asked, if Agnes or Mr. O. saw him? They were his parents, after all. They loved him; they didn't want to hurt him. That wasn't the issue, he said. It wouldn't be right for them or anyone else to see him, it wouldn't be proper or natural: their stares and their touch would burn right through him. I wanted to argue with him, of course, but I could sense in his tone of voice that he really didn't want to discuss it. So I shut up.

As for myself, I was doing ok. I worked hard but the tips were good, and I felt confident again, independent again. My mom's death had created a void in my life, a big, gaping canyon that I filled with work and more work and occasionally a chat with Adam, suddenly my best friend.

Since the funeral, I had kept my bedroom curtains drawn. Adam could no longer watch me sleep. I had grown tired of invisible caresses, tired of angels. I was afraid Adam would ask me why I had suddenly shut him out, but he never said a word.

Our post-midnight chats stopped around June. It had nothing to do with Adam. He was still my friend, but I had started dating one of the waiters at Charlie's, a good-looking guy named Gabriel Chesson, and so I saw very little of Adam; in fact, I was rarely home, preferring Gabriel's more modern apartment to my mom's house with its flowery wallpaper, Chinese vases, and goofy knickknacks from eastern Europe.

8

IN THE SPRING OF 1974, CHARLIE'S GRILLE BURNED to the ground, and I was without a job again. Mr. Glowac, who had become a good friend and mentor and, until I bought my own car, my chauffeur, said he'd try to bring me along with him to O'Malley's. But by the summer Gabriel and I eloped. I sold my mom's house to a family from Maine, and with the money, Gabriel and I drove to Florida to look at restaurant properties outside Orlando. And bingo, in a matter of weeks we were restaurant owners. It all happened so quickly. It kind of took my breath away.

When I told Adam about Gabriel and our plans to go to Florida, he said he wasn't surprised and wished us the best of luck. Then he blurted out that I was the most beautiful woman he had ever seen and that he had made dozens and dozens of drawings of me. I blew him a kiss across the walkway and said good night. The next day, per Adam's instructions, Agnes gave me the address of his former tutor in Florida and suggested that I drop by one day. I never did. I never kept in touch with Adam either. The Orlando restaurant failed, but the restaurant that moved in *after us* was a huge success. I ended up working there as a waitress.

WANDA

1

WHEN I SAW ADAM'S FACE IN HIS BEDROOM window one morning, I was suddenly madly in love with him. I didn't know why and still don't. I'd worked at 7 Peru Street forever, it seemed, and in all that time I never once thought about the young man in the room upstairs. He wasn't a presence or poltergeist or phantom or anything like that. He was just a name, Adam, faceless, bodyless and, for most of us at Pie Man Pies, voiceless. But when I saw him, everything changed. Love at first sight. Just like in the movies. No reason to question or analyze it or doubt it. Which, of course, was the kind of passive attitude that drove Daddy nuts and sometimes saddened him.

Daddy said I wasn't like other girls. He said I was lethargic and careless and disinterested in life, and I guess he was right. I was bashful and awkward, too. Others made fun of me. But that didn't bother me that much. I never really paid attention to them. Or myself. I was what I was and that was that. It was only my attraction to Adam that led me to think that maybe I might want to change the way I looked and acted. I knew I was a mystery to Mrs. Olszewska and the girls in her kitchen, but I kind of liked that. It's nice to be considered mysterious every now and then. But I also knew I was invisible to Adam and that I didn't like at all.

My feelings for Adam took me by surprise. I lived in the apartment over Daddy's store and was walking to work (only about a hundred yards away) and happened to glance up at the second-floor windows at 7 Peru. I knew which one was Adam's. The middle one. It was his bedroom, where he spent all of his time, morning, noon, and night. That window was always dark, the shade always drawn, the curtains, off-white and gauzy, always closed, although a number of times I thought I saw a face or shadow in the window frame, Adam himself, I supposed, looking down at the walkway, maybe even at me on my way to work.

Why did I glance up at Adam's window? Who could resist? There was a real, bona fide hermit behind those curtains, a man completely afraid of everything I took for granted, of walking the street and breathing fresh air in the company of schoolkids and people going to work. He was the kind of freak some people would pay money to see, so I looked up at his window. And Jesus there he was! I could see his face as plain as day, although the more I looked the less clear the face became until it kind of turned into a bunch of shadows or spots of darkness or something. But I did see him. I did. His face was lean and handsome with dark eyes and dark, thick eyebrows. He had high cheekbones and his ears were flat against his head, not sticking out like my Dumbo ears. He had a little beard, a neat little goatee, and looked very artistic, especially with his long black hair, longer than mine and straight. I had to iron my hair, dirty blonde, to get it that straight.

I stopped dead in my tracks, mouth open, absolutely stunned. So what did I, big dope, do? I waved at him. There I was in the middle of the walkway waving at a house! But I wanted to show him that I had seen him, that he had made contact. My heart was pounding like crazy and I started to sweat like I was in gym class. That instant I decided I wanted Adam Olszewski to be a normal young man, able to live in the world like everybody else. And I wanted him to be mine.

He must have ducked behind the curtains because, as I said, his face seemed to dissolve into dark shapes and shadows. I kind of woke up and walked to the end of the walkway, hung a right through the currant bush, opened the screen door to the kitchen, and went in. I wanted to spend as much time with Adam as I possibly could, but I knew that was going to be pretty much impossible. He was a prisoner in that house. Even his own mother hadn't seen his face in over twenty years. To me that was craziness. How could you not see your own son's face for that long? If I were Mrs. I would have busted down the door. I would have grabbed him by the ears and forced him to look at me. I would have kissed him a million times a day.

The other kitchen girls didn't talk about Adam, didn't exhibit any curiosity whatsoever. Mrs. and Danuta mentioned him only now and then and usually it was about the time back in the day when he could step out into the world without fear of being harmed or tainted or defiled or whatever. Actually, there wasn't really much to talk about, was there? What could Mrs. say? My Adam stayed in his room today. He read a book. He read a magazine. He watched TV or listened to London or Paris on his short wave. The only one of us who ever really talked to him was the Polish girl, Betsy, but she was long gone. Her friend Helena was real spooked by Adam and just the mention of his name made her jittery, and for the rest of the day she'd keep looking behind her as if Adam might swoop down on her like a big owl. The two Italian girls thought he was part crazy man, part holy man, part government spy, and they were in awe of him and maybe a little afraid of him, too. He used to have a tutor they called Miss T. and she spent all day upstairs talking at the door to his room, which was, when you think about it, completely nuts. Miss T. left in 1970, a few years after I started working for Mrs. She was very smart but very strange too. At first I thought of her as an enemy, just another someone to make fun of me and laugh at me, but I learned to like her because she never teased me and, more than anyone else, she seemed honestly interested in what I had to say. But after she took off to start her music school, Adam stayed holed up in his room doing who knows what. I knew he spent a lot of his time watching over the neighborhood, including Daddy's market where I lived, in the same upstairs rooms Betsy and Helena used to live in (I moved in the month after Betsy left, walking to work instead of driving Mommy's car in from the suburbs). I knew from Mrs. and young Alex next door that nothing happened in the neighborhood without Adam knowing about it. I also learned from them and from my own observations that Adam was friends with the glamorous Angela Wrobel, the woman across the walkway who had come back from California. Her mother, old Mrs. Wrobel, died a few months before I first saw Adam in the window. Young Alex, who was in high school, said that Angela waited tables at Charlie's Grille, where his dad worked as a bartender, driving Angela to and from the restaurant each night, at least for a while. Alex was a real chatterbox and said he was profoundly in love with Angela, Miss Hollywood herself, and said that Adam probably was too. He said Adam and Angela sometimes talked to each other late at night when Angela got home from work.

"On the telephone?" I asked.

"No, outside. Adam hides in the cucumber vines so she can't see him."

"You mean he was outside his room? And outside this house?"

"That's right," said young Alex. "I've seen him late at night a couple of times."

I wondered if young Alex was leading me up the garden path. I mean, why would he tell me the truth? He wasn't profoundly in love with me, at least I didn't think he was (unless he was profoundly in love with every girl he met), and he was a mischievous little devil with that big brain of his and impish half smile.

So there I was, in love with a hermit, thinking how uncomplicated that would be, only to learn that maybe it wasn't the least bit uncomplicated. In fact, it could end up being a big mess. As soon as love entered my life, jealousy came with it, its sidekick and shadow. Yes, of course I was jealous of Angela even if what Alex said was just a joke. Who wouldn't be? I'd seen her on my lunch break sunbathing in her backyard, barely wearing anything at all. I knew how beautiful she was. Everyone did. But that was only jealousy in the abstract, plain me jealous of glamorous her. But to think that she and Adam might be meeting under the cover of darkness, well, that was too much.

The thing was I was also jealous of Betsy and Miss T. and even of Alex, the little pipsqueak. He was smart as a whip and Adam thought the world of him and the pair of them chatted like magpies whenever Alex visited after school.

And me? I lived on Mars.

2

ONE OF THE ITALIAN GIRLS SAID ADAM WAS A SPY who worked for the Soviet government. His room, she said, was like the New England headquarters for some kind of socialist agency and was filled with cameras and tape recorders and strange machines with blinking lights. I asked if she had any evidence and all she said was, "Just look around." I was beginning to see that Adam wasn't the only nutcase at 7 Peru Street.

3

I SOON DECIDED THAT MY ATTRACTION TO ADAM was getting me nowhere. What's the point of adoring someone when you don't do anything about it? I was being my usual passive self and for once I hated it. But I vowed that this time things were going to be different. I was going to take charge of my life in general and my lovelife in particular. I was going to make a change in the way Adam saw me and the way I saw myself. In fact, I wouldn't be myself anymore. I would be another smarter, craftier person. I would be like Adam, a spy hiding in the shadows. And more than that, I was going to find my way into Adam's heart. I was going to look the man I was madly in love with straight in the eyes.

Not long after that momentous decision, I noticed something very interesting. I was on my way to work, walking past the cukes, slipping through the currant bushes that opened into the backyard, and climbing the porch steps that led to the kitchen door. But that day I spotted a little white thing in the mulch that encircled a dwarf azalea. It was a cigarette butt. That's odd, I thought. No one smoked in the house. Mrs. used to, but she'd given it up years before. Danuta didn't, Mr. didn't, the Italian sisters didn't, I didn't. It must be Adam, I thought. Then it occurred to me. If Adam smoked this butt, then Alex was telling the truth. Adam must have been outside. He must have left the confines of his room. And he must have chatted with Angela during the wee hours. That instant I knew what I had to do.

On a Friday in June 1973, I pretended to go home after work. I said good night to Mrs. and Danuta and the sisters and walked out the kitchen door. But instead of following the cobblestone path that led to Peru Street, I reentered the house through the front door and hid in the closet under the stairwell that led to Adam's room. I left the closet door open a crack to allow in light, and I stayed there, crouched on the floor, hidden from view by jackets and coats. I remained awake through dinner listening to Mr. and Mrs. chat about this and that.

Then Mrs. brought Adam his meal. Then the two of them went upstairs to visit with Adam, their footsteps just inches from the top of my head. Then they came downstairs again and went into the den to watch TV. That was when I took a little nap. When I woke up it was two in the morning. Mr. and Mrs. were upstairs asleep. I listened for Adam, but couldn't hear anything. I sneaked out of the closet and walked as quietly as I could into the kitchen. The door to the backyard was open. I saw Adam sitting on the back steps. Had he already talked with Angela? Was he going to? Who knew? Maybe those late-night blab sessions that Alex told me about were already a thing of the past. When I saw him (I was in the kitchen hiding behind one of the pie ovens) he was smoking a cigarette and listening to a small radio with the volume really low.

I watched him for a while, then I tiptoed back up the stairs, hoping the door to Adam's bedroom was open. It was. I went in. It was amazing. I was actually in Adam's room, his inner sanctum. I spent the rest of the night crouched like a stowaway in a dark corner of the room, hiding in a space between a bureau and a wall, just wide enough so I could fit and just dark enough so I couldn't be seen. I waited for him to come to bed. I looked around the room, trying to memorize it, I guess. The only light came from a floor lamp next to a green easy chair. I saw a large radio, a short-wave, I think, a console TV, and a drawing table like in an architectural firm or something. The walls were covered top to bottom with shelves holding books and magazines and other stuff. From my position in the corner of the room behind a chest, it looked like I was in a library or book store.

But there weren't any machines with blinking lights, no CIA spying devices. Nothing even close. And so I was right. The Italian girls were nuts.

My plan was to sneak out and leave for home after he fell asleep, but since he didn't sleep at all that night my only chance for escape came very early in the morning when he went to the bathroom. Adam spent nearly the entire night in his green chair either looking out the window or reading from a thin little book called *The Death of a Nobody* and writing little notes in the margins. It was amazing. He was even better looking than he'd been when I saw him in the windowpane. He wasn't just cute, he was stunningly handsome. It seemed even crazier than ever that someone as gorgeous as he was would confine himself to his room for life. What a waste, I thought. But then I reconsidered. He was so good looking that if he were out in the regular world, the girls wouldn't leave him alone. He'd be too handsome for the likes of me. I can make myself look very attractive if I have to. But even at my best I couldn't compete for Adam. He was that beautiful. I got soaking wet just looking at him. But all I could do that night was watch. I couldn't just jump up and yell surprise. That would scare him off. He'd hide under the bed or something and think I was out of my mind. I had to be content with being only a few feet away. I could hear him breathing. I could hear him clear his throat. I smelled his cigarette smoke. And I didn't move a muscle.

Since it was Saturday morning when I got home that first time, I didn't have to worry about work. I left 7 Peru when the sky was just turning blue. I walked to Daddy's store and climbed up the back stairs to the rooms where I grew up. I eased myself into bed but I was too excited for sleep. When it was light out, I heard someone open the back door to the market downstairs. I looked out the window and saw an old Ford pickup parked in the driveway. It was Pawel. Daddy had hired him a few months before and he seemed to be working out to everyone's satisfaction. Daddy liked him because he knew the retail business and he knew about marketing and such things. In fact, now that Pawel worked at the market, Daddy rarely came in anymore. He and Mommy lived in their new house with a weathervane on the roof and a horse barn across the road and a garden in the center of their backyard.

Pawel came in the back way, passing the cutting table. I rarely saw him or got the chance to talk with him. I was usually busy making pies when he opened the market at eight, and he was usually busy with customers or cutting meats or doing the books or some other thing when I got home from 7 Peru. He was a big man with short black hair that looked painted on his head. He seemed oafish all right, but he surprised people by how graceful he could be, and his voice wasn't rough at all for a big man. Even though it was a deep voice, it had a gentle purring quality to it like he was trying to hypnotize you. Daddy said that Pawel was very popular with the customers. He was a big friendly bear and he was polite and helpful. Still, the market was losing money because the big stores were underselling us and a lot of our customers went to them to save. They left Daddy even though he was so good about giving them credit and letting them repay what they owed when they could. Mrs. didn't leave us though. She said Shop&Save was too big for her and it made her dizzy and it smelled of ammonia.

I went over to the top of the staircase and had a view of most of the market, but without being seen. Pawel was bringing a large plate filled with hams and sausages from the fridge to the showcase. He was big but not fat. He was thick as a tree with a neck like a football player's, and his hands were thick and looked like they were made of stone. He wore some kind of high school ring on his right hand and a religious medal around his neck. I guessed that he was probably twice my weight.

4

I STAYED THAT MONDAY NIGHT AT THE OLSZEWSKI house. I was the invisible girl again. I went where I pleased, seeing and unseen. I brought a change of clothes with me, which I kept in the front closet, and I also brought along a dopp kit filled with toiletries and things in case I couldn't escape. When Adam sneaked outside for his late night smoke (he didn't chat with Angela as far as I could tell), I went into his room and slipped naked into his bed. The warmth of it, his warmth, excited me. I started to masturbate. I couldn't help myself. I had an orgasm in record time. Then I went to my corner of the bedroom and waited for Adam to come back.

When he returned he sat in his green chair, reading his book and listening to a symphony from Prague or somewhere on his short wave. Eventually he went to bed. It was around four in the morning, maybe five. He slept soundly and snored a little. I loved the way he snored, a kind of low-pitched bird call. I sneaked up on him when he was in a deep sleep and sat on the edge of his bed for a few minutes. I even touched him on the forehead, hoping I wouldn't disturb him. Then I left his room and went into the den and watched the late late late late show. I ate a slice of a pie I'd helped make the morning before. I cut a very narrow slice so nobody would see that a night visitor had been in the house. I knew it was risky, but I didn't care. I felt really weird. Nothing that could happen to me could bother me.

When Mr. and Mrs. came down the stairs at six or so, I was long gone, already home washing up and getting ready to start work at eight. That day I started to become more like Adam. I was no longer shy, sleepy Wanda, but smart, mysterious Wanda. I decided to read more too, knowing that Adam would like that. I wasn't very good at it, but I tried anyway, thinking that maybe one day soon I could use reading and books as an excuse to talk with him. I barely passed my last year of high school and then I came to work in Mrs.'s kitchen, part time, then full-time. Daddy wanted me to quit Pie Man Pies and work in the market, but I didn't want to do that. What would I do all day but stand around waiting on a bunch of old ladies? Of course I knew Daddy had matchmaking plans for me and Pawel, and I guess I ruined them for him, but not entirely. I mean, I was living above where Pawel worked so there was still hope for Daddy, although I didn't tell him about my mad love affair with Adam. He wouldn't have understood at all.

That same afternoon I told Mrs. that I wanted to attend the community college in the fall and wondered if I could borrow some books from Adam. She looked at me and smiled and told me to go upstairs and ask him myself. I did as she suggested and went upstairs, but I couldn't find the courage to knock on the door. It was too weird. A few hours before I'd been on the other side of that door. I had climaxed in Adam's bed. I had touched him ever so lightly and gently.

The next night I entered his room grinning like a fool because I knew every inch of the place. I knew where everything belonged. I knew where Adam slept. I'd seen his piles of drawings, none of me though, at least none that I could see. I returned to my spot in the shadows, and when he came in the room he sat in his green chair and opened his book.

At around four in the morning, Adam finally went to sleep. The room was completely dark. I left my spot in the corner, took off my clothes, and carefully lowered myself over his body and opened the fly of his pajama bottoms. I took in his penis whole and waited for his erection to fill my mouth. He woke up immediately, of course. I mean, imagine how it must have felt having me descend on him like a fog and end his twenty-something years of celibacy. He tried to jump out of bed, but then decided better of it and settled back, feeling this incredible pleasure, but not having the slightest idea of what it was exactly or who was causing it. I wondered if he thought he was still dreaming. And yet he must have felt the solidness of his mattress and felt my hot breath as I hovered over him. Of course it was too dark to tell who was who and what was what. Finally he figured out it was me. He was ready to stop everything, but then he heard a low moan in my throat, and he felt the heat of my quickening breath and felt the whip of my hair and he let go. Sperm City. It was a real flood all right, a river from him to me. I thought he must want more, but he didn't at all. He rolled out of his bed, landed on the floor, and made a dash for his bathroom, closing the door behind him and leaving me alone and naked on his bed. Now there was *another* door I had to deal with. I went over to it, knocked on it, whispered to Adam that he'd really like it a lot if he came out, but he didn't. He didn't even speak. I thought I might have done something wrong and so I said I was sorry. I didn't mean to hurt him. I wanted to make him feel good. I mean I was nuts about him. It wasn't like I had raped him. I mean, girls didn't rape boys, did they?

The next day on my lunch break, I told Mrs. I was going to talk to Adam about the books I should read for community college. I went upstairs and tried to open the door. It was locked. I gently knocked and said I was ready to continue where I had left off the night before. I didn't expect a reply and when I got one it nearly floored me. He said he didn't want to hurt my feelings, but he couldn't have sex with me again. Well, I said, didn't you enjoy yourself? There was a long period of silence. Yes, he said finally, he did. He said he liked it because I was kind of a disembodied thing floating over him. It gave him pleasure because there was only a single point of contact, because our bodies never really touched and because we were in the dark and I couldn't hurt him. I didn't know what he was talking about. He tried to explain a bit more, but to be honest I wasn't really listening to what he said. I was flabbergasted that he was actually talking to me. I thought that maybe he really didn't mind my early morning visit. I wondered if he was saying no no no when he really meant yes yes yes. We talked about how I managed to invade his room, his inner sanctum, so I let him know all my tricks. Staying overnight, hiding in the closet, everything. Then, as a way to keep him engaged, I asked him about community college and what books I should be reading, and he said, in a kinder voice and one without an edge to it, that he would be delighted to help me with my studies just as he had helped Betsy. At one point he even started to explain to me why he was a hermit and how the house had this weird power over him. Finally, I asked if he would tell his mother about my visit, which, if he did, meant I would soon be out of a job. He said he had no intention of telling his mother or anyone else.

The next few days at around four o'clock, or whenever, I made my usual circle from back door to front, and then remained crouched for hours in the front closet, waiting for early morning when Adam left his room for a smoke. But he never left his room. I went upstairs and tried his door. It was locked. I knocked and knocked and knocked, not caring if I woke up Mr. and Mrs. or the whole neighborhood. But he wouldn't acknowledge me. He didn't even have the courtesy or courage or whatever to tell me to get lost.

I decided this was nuts. I wasn't going to spend my nights in a cramped little closet waiting for Adam to talk to me, to welcome me into his life or even just into his room. The last night I stayed over I decided at around four in the morning to stop waiting for him to acknowledge my existence. I decided to go home. I was too upset and too wired to sleep, so instead I showered and dressed and watched the *Today* show for a little while waiting until seven. Then I sat barefoot at the top of the staircase/ladder in the back of the store and watched Pawel get the store ready for business. His skin was rosy brown, which meant he'd recently been at the beach, maybe even that weekend. That was something we had in common. I really loved going to the beach even though my skin was fair and I had to spend most of my time there covered up or under an umbrella. When I was little, my parents took me to the beach in Rhode Island and I had fun swimming in the ocean. Sometimes the waves would be very high, and Daddy and I would dig our toes into the sand and wait for the waves to knock us over, and we'd laugh and laugh as we got to our feet again in the hissing foam. Then we'd all go out to dinner at a restaurant overlooking the ocean and I'd have scallops, and Mommy, of course, would have a Bloody Mary before the meal and then a second after the salad and then a third with the main course, and Daddy would order bluefish coated with mayonnaise and then baked, which wasn't on the menu, but the chef made it special for him, although I have to say the smell of that fish couldn't be covered up with mayonnaise or anything else. It was really overpowering, but I didn't mind it. It was the smell of the sea. The smell of life and death mixed into one.

I watched Pawel carefully. He was really just like Daddy, all business, and I knew for a fact Daddy had something sneaky in mind when he hired him. He wanted us to meet and date and fall in love and get married and have kids. Why else were we so close together with me living upstairs and him working down? Why else would he always ask me how Pawel was doing like I was dating him? Daddy was shameless playing the matchmaker and meddling in my life, and he couldn't say enough about his precious Pawel, how organized he was and how he had streamlined the books, and he started sales promotions so customers would come in on slow days. I leaned over a bit and could see him paging through the books, making entries here and there and looking very serious. Then he went on to trimming various cuts of beef and I started thinking how good looking he was in a truck driver kind of way and how his big forearms twitched when he trimmed away the fat. I noticed he had a small tattoo on his right forearm. It was a little banner with the word JOY in it, and I wondered if Joy was the name of a former girlfriend or if it was, you know, just joy. Then I realized it was getting late, and when I glanced at Pawel one last time, he was gone, and I thought he might have slipped into the front of the store to set up the sausages and cheese or something, and then I heard the *snip snip snip* of scissors and saw his wide smiling face at the same level as my feet. He said that maybe he should add a few little piggies to his sausage, meaning my toes. I didn't say anything. Instead I gave him my hand and he took it and I pulled him toward me up the stairs and into my bedroom and when we reached my bed I felt dizzy and warm and solid. And before I knew it he was on top of me and it felt like I was being covered by the whole world.

5

FROM THAT DAY ON, I WENT HOME RIGHT AFTER work. I went upstairs and showered and got the flour out of my hair and waited for Pawel to close the store, which was usually at six. Sometimes I made him dinner, sometimes we went out to dinner. Sometimes we skipped dinner altogether and spent the night in bed.

After a while I couldn't believe I was once crazy about Adam. I think that maybe I was just crazy. I didn't think about him anymore, not a single thought. It was like that night when I hovered over him never even happened. I decided that the last thing I wanted was to be like Adam, a hermit stuck in a chair, reading books and stuff. What crap. I wanted to be myself and I wanted Pawel to be himself and that was that.

At work, I never even went near the stairs that led up to Adam's room. Then one day Mrs. came up to me and said that Adam had left me some books to read. She said she was glad that I was still interested in going to the community college. Well, I wasn't interested at all, but I kept that to myself and told her to thank Adam for me.

"Well, thank him yourself," she said and wouldn't leave until she saw me climb those stairs and heard me knock on Adam's door. He asked who was there, and when I said Wanda his voice became hushed and maybe a little quivery, as if he was nervous or tense or something. I thanked him for the books and he said you're welcome. To be honest, I didn't even look at them. They could have been written in French for all I knew. He then offered to help me if I had any troubles with my studies. Maybe I was hearing things, but I sensed a sadness in his voice. Maybe it was regret that I sensed. Maybe he wanted to be with me again, wanted to go back to that night when I invaded his room and had sex with him in the darkness. Oh, I knew he knew about Pawel. He knew about everything in the neighborhood. He'd probably seen Pawel dozens of times in the early morning and had heard that the neighborhood really liked him and that he was helpful and nice and had an excellent sense of humor. Adam must have seen Pawel's truck in the market driveway all night long, and he must have imagined me in my bed hovering over Pawel's naked body and the thought of it must have made him feel ill the way you feel ill when you miss out on something you could've easily had. I sensed that he wished I would come back to him and I sensed that he would promise me that things would be different. We wouldn't be disembodied lovers. We wouldn't hide in the darkness. We'd make love like humans, not ghosts. Was I imagining it all? Probably. But listening to him offer to help me study, I had the feeling he knew he had underestimated and misunderstood me. He knew now I wasn't just some silly girl. There was a lot more to me and he had somehow missed it all.

6

A FEW MONTHS LATER I ANNOUNCED TO MRS. and the girls that I had decided to leave Pie Man Pies and work with Pawel at Daddy's market, and then, with a sly grin, I added that Pawel and I were engaged to be married in October and lifted my hand to show off my engagement ring. It so impressed the sisters they couldn't take their eyes off it the entire morning. Mrs. congratulated me and said I would be sorely missed, but I knew she was just being polite and, while it's true that I did whatever I was told and never talked back or resisted or came in late or left early, I knew I was her least favorite worker. In her mind I had no spirit, no zip. She had the same opinion of me that Daddy did.

I wondered if Mrs. knew anything about Adam and me. Maybe she saw how I'd acted like a goof during those few days, all moony and dreamy, as if I had some kind of schoolgirl crush. Oh well. It really didn't matter anymore.

Pawel and I were married on a beautiful October day in 1973. Almost everyone in the neighborhood was invited, including everyone at Pie Man Pies, Adam too. And everyone, except Adam, came to the ceremony at St. Paul's and the reception that followed at the K-Club. The sisters and most of the neighbors stayed late into the night dancing and drinking beer while Mr. and Mrs. and Danuta and her man left an hour or so after dinner. I was told that Adam remained in his room with his window open so he could hear the buzz of voices from the reception and listen to the music. I was also told that Mrs. came home in an exceptionally good mood because the caterer, my Uncle Sal, had insisted on serving Pie Man Pies for dessert. Mrs. had filled the order free of charge the day before as a wedding gift, and she was pleased when people said that hers were the best pies they'd ever tasted. At the reception I gave Mrs. a huge hug and thanked her for the pies, then I said how much I would miss everyone and as I glided away I added: "And Adam too."

Two years later, Pawel called Mrs. and told her that Pie Man Pies hadn't been selling at the normal rate at the market and that we'd have to lower our standing order to five pies daily. More and more of our customers were going to the big supermarkets where they could get pies for a fraction of the price. We couldn't afford to sell the pies at discount, much less give them away to the old people as Mrs. had insisted early on. One late afternoon in 1975, Daddy and I visited Mrs. and told her that the market was closing down. Daddy confessed that the market had not been terribly profitable during the last few years, and it had been kept afloat almost entirely because of Pawel and the ingenuity of his bookkeeping and sales promotions and his popularity with the customers. On the positive side, I mentioned that Pawel had found a job as a meatcutter at Shop&Save, which Daddy said was ironic, but ironic or not it was good news to me because I was pregnant and expected to deliver that winter. Pawel and I had already moved out of the upstairs rooms, which were now vacant, and lived in an apartment downtown.

The next week Pawel left for Shop&Save and Daddy came out of retirement to guide his market through its last days. He no longer sold Pie Man Pies, but as Mrs. had suggested, he told his few remaining customers that if they phoned her and gave her a day's notice, they could order pies from Mrs. herself and Mr. Laver would gladly add them to his list of deliveries. Soon the market was nothing more than an empty room with empty shelves and empty showcases and empty meat freezers and refrigerators. Over the cutting table hung a pristine curlycue of golden flypaper—even the flies had abandoned the place. Eventually, Daddy sold the property to a man who thought that a retail operation wasn't feasible in that kind of neighborhood and turned the store and the upstairs rooms into a duplex that Pawel and I actually looked at a few years later, but we wanted something more in the country.

DR. COHEN

USUALLY, THE LONGER YOU SEE A PATIENT THE better you know him or her. That was decidedly not the case with Adam Olszewski. I knew him best when he was a little boy who hated to go to school. In the years that followed, I knew less and less about him until I reached a point where I knew nothing at all.

Adam was a man without a personality, without a psychology: instead, he was a living enigma, a permanent and unanswerable question. I have my theories, of course, and other medical people I know, once I told them what I knew, had theirs as well. But the theories were just clouds, puffs of smoke. I won't even bother to review them. They're not important. What is important is that Adam's parents refused to let him be admitted into a care facility. They didn't want their boy to be taken away from them, fearing the worst. Do I blame them? No, I don't. They had a kind of old-country mistrust of authority; they didn't even trust people who wanted to help them, me included. They liked me and I liked them, but I could never get them to part with their child in a million years. Do I think they made the right decision? Who knows? If Agnes and Teddy allowed me to institutionalize young Adam, things might have turned out differently; perhaps it might have been an excruciating ordeal for the boy, but it's possible that, at the end of it, my colleagues and I could have turned his life around and set him on a path toward normalcy. Then again, we might have done him irreparable harm or driven him to harm others. Maybe it was really all a crapshoot after all and maybe Agnes and Teddy did, in truth, make the right decision.

Adam's case was so severe and so peculiar that, after his seventh birthday, I wasn't allowed to examine the boy anymore. After his parents and I filmed him to show that he was visibly and undeniably housebound, I couldn't even take his temperature or give him a needle (luckily he already had all his shots, including polio). I protested vigorously, but Agnes and Teddy (mostly Agnes) thought it best to obey Adam's wishes and leave him alone. But what if there was a medical emergency? I asked. What if he had a seizure? Would they let him lapse into unconsciousness or live in pain?

No, no, said Teddy. He'd bust down the door, he said.

I believed him, of course, and I was glad to hear him say what he said, since I was convinced that one day he or Agnes would call me and say the boy was burning up with fever or suffering from terrible chills or had broken his arm or was having nightmares. But you know what? That never happened. Adam's childhood was without illness and without troubles, which sounds amazing but, if you think about it, it makes a lot of sense, too, since he never came in contact with germ-ridden children. Or, after a while, with anyone. He was living in a vacuum, so to speak. After all, what is childhood but the endless exchange of viruses and bacteria?

During those early years of Adam's self-imposed captivity, I was a fairly frequent visitor at 7 Peru Street. Those were the days when doctors made house calls, you see. But soon things fell into a routine that didn't include me. A tutor was hired, a perky, talented young woman, and gradually Adam's young life seemed to achieve its own brand of normalcy. He was a bright, healthy, polite little boy who happened to live in a single room and who couldn't abide the presence and gaze of others. Later, my visits to the house were more limited, maybe once or twice a year. I'd talk to Agnes and Teddy, but they never told me anything about Adam. That's because they didn't know anything. They said he sounded happy and content, but that was the extent of their evaluation. I ended up going upstairs and interviewing him through his bedroom door, but he wasn't terribly cooperative. He answered me, if he answered at all, in monosyllables. As I said, he wouldn't let me examine him and when I asked him if anything bothered him, if he had any pain or discomfort or if he experienced sadness or regret, he said he was fine.

Actually, my visits were mostly of a social nature. I'd drop by when I was in the neighborhood, knowing full well that a healthy slice of one of Agnes's astonishing pies was waiting for me. Even when Adam was a fully grown man nothing really changed. Life went on as usual in the Olszewski household. Everything was fine and dandy. Oh well. All I know is that whenever I thought of that young man and his family, every time I saw that house, every time I thought of the little boy who couldn't step into his own backyard, I felt a profound sadness in my heart. What a waste of a mind! When he was a boy I thought he was constantly trying to outsmart his parents and me, faking illness in order to stay home from school, that sort of thing. The tragedy is that maybe he got what he wanted and when he got it, when he attained perfect security in his room, he didn't know how to unget it. He was stuck. He outsmarted everyone, including himself, and gained nothing for it. What did he lose? He lost his life.

THADDEUS

1

NEITHER ADAM NOR I KNEW RIGHT AWAY WHAT happened on January 23, 1981. I was at work and Adam was, as always, in his room reading or keeping his eye on the neighborhood.

On January 20, Agnes had received a phone call from a Mr. Terrence, who introduced himself as vice president of development at Shop&Save. He said he had heard some very good things about Pie Man Pies and wondered if he and Agnes could meet for lunch, his treat, of course, at Vitolini's restaurant downtown. He said he could help expand the Pie Man Pies business in a way that would be profitable for her and for Shop&Save. Agnes agreed and they set a lunch date for January 23, her birthday. That night I planned to make dinner for her and give her a lovely emerald ring that I had bought for her at the jewelers up the street from Witold's variety store.

Danuta and the sisters said that Agnes was a little nervous getting ready for her meeting, fixing her hair just so, deciding which silk blouse went best with her gray suit and then which necklace went best with her silk blouse. She left the house at 11:30 with the women telling her how good she looked ("like a movie star," Zosia said) and making sure there was no flour dust on her shoulders and skirt. She returned a few minutes later saying that the car battery had died and immediately called for a taxi, explaining to the dispatcher that she was in a hurry and had a very important business meeting to attend. She was really nervous, the women said, but just then they heard a horn toot outside. The cabby had been only a few minutes away, on the corner of Bolivia and Peru, when he got the dispatch.

As to what happened next, I have Mr. Terrence himself as a source. He spent a long time talking with me, making sure I knew exactly what had transpired during the hour he and Agnes had spent together. He said he had expected Agnes to be late since there was still snow on the ground and the streets were still slushy and slippery, but there she was, striding into the dining area precisely at noon. Mr. Terrence, a large, balding man, stood up when he saw her, and when he extended his large soft hand Agnes shook it vigorously, prompting him to say she had the grip of a longshoreman. She laughed and then gave him the pie she'd been carrying with her.

When they sat down to lunch, Agnes unwisely ordered baked ziti, unwisely because with the second forkful she splattered her skirt with red sauce (my wife had lovely manners but no one was more accident-prone at the table). She covered the stain with her napkin and hoped Mr. Terrence didn't noticed it. He did, of course, but he said nothing. They began talking business, specifically pie production. In his mind, the only real issue was whether Pie Man Pies could handle increasing production by a factor of ten or more, maybe a lot more. And if Pie Man Pies caught on in Silverton, he said, other Shop&Saves would come on board, stores all over New England. That would mean using commercial ovens, which Agnes did not want to do. Agnes argued that it was, in part, using small ovens that made her pies taste homemade.

"This is not a time to think small," Mr. Terrence told Agnes. "Pie Man Pies will put out a quality pie, as homemade as they come, but our goal is to make the best pie under the given circumstances and make money doing it."

For dessert, Mr. Terrence said he and Agnes each had a generous slice of her French apple pie. He admitted to me that he had had seconds and entertained the idea of having thirds. After they were done eating, they exchanged business cards and shook hands again; then Mr. Terrence left the restaurant, taking what remained of the pie with him. Agnes stayed a while longer to finish her coffee and then left in a cab. No doubt she was still upset about the tomato stain on her skirt.

The taxi must have gone down Olive Street, then turned the corner onto Jefferson. It must have slowed down, because it was approaching the railroad tracks that divided the city in two. Near the railroad station was Witold's variety store. He told me that he happened to glance out the front window of his store and saw a huge dump truck rumbling down Jefferson at a deadly rate of speed. Clouds of thick white smoke surged from the truck's wheels. The driver had stuck his head out of the window and was screaming. The sound, Witold said, was harrowing, a howl from the world of the dead. My friend ran into the street and saw the truck, three cars away from the taxi, coming at it from the opposite direction. It soon demolished and pushed aside the first car, then the second. Instead of striking the third car, the truck veered off to the right but, an instant later, swerved left again and, somehow gaining speed, climbed up over the taxi's hood. Its left front wheel, huge and black, threads spewing mud and stone and snow, crushed the windshield and roof.

Witold and a group of bystanders made their way to the heap of smashed metal and broken glass hoping to find someone alive. A few people were hideously mangled and beyond hope, but most were alive. When Witold came to the taxi he discovered that the driver was dead, but the woman in the back seat was breathing, although the left side of her was pinned under the truck tire. To his horror he realized that the woman was Agnes. When she opened her eyes, Witold said, she seemed to recognize him. He called out to her:

"Agnieszka! Agnieszka! Are you in pain?"

"Is that you, Tadek?" she said, thinking it was me standing over her.

"No, no, it's me, Witold, your friend."

She nodded her head yes as if she understood. She said she felt numb and tired, very tired. She said her head weighed a hundred pounds and so she let it drop, her eyes focused now on her gray skirt, which had climbed halfway up her thighs. Witold noticed that she was staring at what appeared to be a tomato sauce stain, more brown now than red. She told him its shape was like one of the countries in Adam's maps. Witold, of course, didn't know what she was talking about. He told her he would call the Aircraft to get in touch with me. Then he repeated her name again and again, but each time he said it she seemed farther and farther away. Then my dear friend noticed another stain, this one on her blouse under her suit jacket. It was located below the collar, already a large circle, but no longer growing any larger, brilliant red at first but, like the sauce, turning brown.

2

WHEN I TOLD ADAM WHAT HAD HAPPENED, there was a terrible silence on the other side of the door. Then I heard sobbing. I knocked again and again, calling out my son's name, begging him to open the door, to look at me and allow me to look at him, to embrace, for goodness sake.

"Your mother is gone," I cried out. "All we have now is each other. We have to start a new life together. The old way, with you locked in your room, has to give way. How can I grieve with you, how can I love you when I can't even look at you?"

I continued along those lines for I don't know how long, but there was no response. All I heard was sobbing but, in truth, I had never heard sobbing like that before. It was the deep, full-throated sobbing of a man, not a boy, a sobbing that came from the deepest levels of the soul and seemed to linger on the verge of gagging and choking and death. I couldn't bear to listen to it. At one point I thought he had stopped, but he hadn't. It was just that my own sobbing had grown so loud I could no longer hear his.

For the first time in my life I hated my son and wished he were swept off the face of the earth.

3

THE NEXT MORNING, I MET WITH DANUTA TO make funeral arrangements. After we were done, I went upstairs to bring Adam a cup of coffee and a piece of blueberry pie that hadn't been delivered the day before. I knocked our secret knock then tried to open the door on my own but, of course, it was locked. When I knocked the second time, I heard Adam wish me a good morning.

"I'm sorry about yesterday," he said. "I didn't mean to hurt you. I want us to begin a new life together as you said, but I have no control over myself. It's like there's someone telling me what to do, what to feel, and I can't disobey, even though I want to very much."

I placed his breakfast on the hallway floor and said I'd return in half an hour. I waited in the kitchen, looking around at the room that, a few days before, had been filled with the noise and chaos of work. Now it was like a morgue. Agnes's three ovens looked absurdly out of place. The oversized bowls and stacks of Pie Man Pies boxes and pie plates were unceremoniously piled in a corner. A large pottery vase in the middle of the kitchen table held the spoons and spatulas and other instruments of piemaking, a bouquet of wooden and stainless steel flowers. I went outside for a while to breathe in the icy January air. I suppose I was still upset with Adam, but I knew it wouldn't last.

When I returned upstairs, Adam's tray was waiting for me: he hadn't touched the pie. I sat in the white wooden chair I had sat in all those years when Agnes and I chatted with him during our post-dinner visits. He must have heard me rumbling around because he said hello and asked if I was all right. I said I wasn't and wouldn't be for a long, long time. He corrected me and said that most likely we wouldn't be all right ever again. Then he asked me how Danuta was doing, and I said she was taking it very hard, which, of course, was to be expected.

I told Adam about the funeral arrangements Danuta and I had made. Agnes was to be cremated, per her wishes, with her ashes scattered in the spring over her beloved backyard tomato garden.

Danuta had suggested a ceremony in the parlor for friends and family and neighbors. Nothing religious. No priests or nuns: not a single one. People would form a line and offer their sympathies and reminiscences in an orderly and reasonable fashion. After the ceremony, everyone would walk down to the K-Club for a reception, which Mr. Kozak's brother-in-law would cater. Agnes had been very pleased at how he managed Wanda and Pawel's wedding, except this time there would be no Pie Man Pies for dessert: Agnes's kitchen would remain quiet for a long time, maybe even forever. I asked Adam what he thought of the plan and he said it was fine with him. Anticipating my question, he added that he would not make an appearance at the ceremony in the parlor, nor would he attend the reception. He would spend the time remembering Agnes in his own way, that is, in his room.

4

ON THE MORNING OF THE RECEPTION, MEN FROM the K-Club brought in portable metal chairs and arranged them in fastidious rows in the parlor. After the ceremony, they returned the chairs to the Club and set them around large tables so people could sit down for a lunch buffet after they finished their drinks at the bar. On a mahogany taboret, I placed a ceramic urn containing Agnes's ashes. On the urn were embossed green leaves, not tomato leaves, but they could, with a little imagination, be taken for them.

People began to arrive at ten. A man from the funeral home that had arranged the cremation opened the front door and asked people to sign a guestbook. He had the wan, hollow look of a recovering alcoholic, but he did his job with an odd enthusiasm and energy, tempering his high spirits with respectfulness and solemnity. Soon the parlor was overflowing with people: neighbors, relatives, friends, my Aircraft coworkers, Club members. At about ten after ten, I kept hoping Adam would make a dramatic entrance, but no such luck. I was the only person in the receiving line.

The first to offer condolences was Wanda, a bit unsteady and looking more and more like her late mother. She was with her husband Pawel, now Paul, his enormous arms wrapped protectively around her shoulders. Then came Mr. Kozak, looking weary and defeated by life, then dear Witold, the last person to see Agnes alive; he broke into tears the instant I embraced him, causing a chain reaction of sorrow throughout the room. Then a school chum of Betsy's introduced herself, a young woman who looked a little like Betsy, solid, indifferent to fashion, even frumpy; she passed along Betsy's deepest condolences from the upper peninsula of Michigan. Next in line were Dr. Cohen (who asked if Adam would make an appearance and only shook his head when I said he wouldn't), Anna Maria and Zosia, Danuta and Alfredo, and a host of neighbors and friends, plus a number of people I didn't know or didn't recognize or didn't remember. Alex's uncle appeared, offering condolences from the Glowac family, who had followed Alex, now a chemistry professor, to California (even Jake had tagged along). One stranger, a large, bald man with prominent jowls and small square teeth (it appeared he lacked canines), turned out to be Mr. Terrence. Later, at the reception, he would spend quite a long time with me recounting his lunch with Agnes.

I had steeled myself to be a good host, to listen graciously to every expression of grief and commiseration, to accept every handshake and tender pat on the shoulder and smile at every comical or charming reminiscence. But I soon discovered that I didn't have to steel myself at all. The good wishes and stories and embraces were like a therapy for me. They didn't negate or mollify my sadness, but I felt that at least I wasn't alone in my grief.

Later, everyone left for the reception at the K-Club. When it was over I came home and climbed the stairs to Adam's room. The door, of course, was closed. He said he had spent the morning in his chair watching his neighbors strolling along the walkway to and from the reception.

"How was it?" he asked.

"It was fine, fine," I replied. "Young Wanda Kozak had too much to drink and had to be taken home by her husband. I met Mr. Terrence, the fellow from Shop&Save who wanted to be your mother's partner. Later on tonight I'll tell you what he told me. I'm too beat right now. A lot of people wondered about the business. Some thought that you should come out of your seclusion and take it over. They said you should be Pie Man to honor your mother's memory. I didn't want to be impolite, so I just said that honoring your mother's memory would never be a problem for you."

I left to take a nap but returned a second later to slip an envelope under the door. It was a letter from Miss T. I went to my room and almost fell into bed I was so tired, but as exhausted as I was, I couldn't sleep. The house was making noises, unusual noises, whooshing sounds, like sighs, as if it were processing Agnes's spirit and sending it into the next world. Either that or else it was dismayed that Adam and I would have to spend so many more nights at the mercy of our grief.

That evening, Adam left the letter from Miss T. on my wooden chair in the hallway. He had scribbled a little note stating that Miss T. had written it for both of us.

Dearest Adam and Mr. O.,

I'm so sorry that I wasn't there for the funeral ceremonies. I suffer from an incredible inertia—clinical depression no doubt—and have begun to be as nervous as a cat about all sorts of things, flying to Connecticut among them. I sit around avoiding my terrible self-satisfied neighbors—naziesque bastards all of them—all you need is greed! But, dearest Adam and dearest Mr. O., proximity has no effect on my sorrow. I've been in a funk ever since I heard the news from Danuta, our wonderfully thoughtful and helpful and delightful friend and once-and-future Agnes-alterego. I've turned into a mope and a dope, bumping into things, trying to remember Mrs. Olszewska, and becoming frustrated because my memories of her—which should be so many—are so few. Why do we drop off memories like old skin cells—or is it just me? All I know is that I must have thousands of memories of Mrs. Olszewska somewhere in my brain and maybe I'll get to retrieve them if I work at it hard enough.

Anyway, I'm writing to tell you the obvious—to ask you to be strong, as strong as Mrs. Olszewska would have been. Oh dear—but it was such a violent horrible way to leave us.

Now things are coming back to me. What I do remember most is how much Mrs. Olszewska liked her Chopin—and eventually my Ravel. If I can claim to have done anything good in this life it's introducing her to the piano music of Maurice Ravel. How she loved the sad birds and the fairy garden. And, you know, our poor Ravel was in a taxi accident, too—in Paris, in the 1930s—and the trauma of it affected his brain so much that in his last years he couldn't think straight, couldn't put a note down on paper. I read where he once wrote a letter like this one—offering condolences to a friend whose mother had passed—and it took him eight days to compose the thing! Mr. Olszewski—you are the loveliest of men. And Adam—you are Pie Man, the spirit of your mother. Be strong—both of you.

Later in the evening, I made Adam and myself spaghetti with tomato sauce from a jar. I ate mine in the hallway—he ate his in his room. Through the door we talked about Pie Man Pies and what he and I were going to do for the rest of our lives. Adam wondered if Pie Man Pies would be *kaput*. I said, yes, it would probably quietly vanish. If Danuta wanted to continue the business, that was fine, but she'd have to do it elsewhere. There was an abandoned bakery on Bolivia Street; maybe, I said, she could go there if the ovens were in decent shape. I'd help clean up the place. I told Adam that I would soon remove the two extra ovens in the kitchen and return the room to the way it was when Adam was a boy, but he said that wasn't necessary. He wanted the kitchen to remain just as it was, with the three ovens intact, a reminder of his mother and her energy and industry and enthusiasm. He hoped that I wouldn't make any other dramatic changes to the house. I said I wouldn't if that was the way he felt about it. To be honest, I also liked the house the way it was, the way Agnes had made it, the home and headquarters of Pie Man Pies.

5

THE URN REMAINED IN THE PARLOR THE ENTIRE winter. We thought it was a good idea to scatter Agnes's ashes a few weeks after Adam's birthday, the time of year when the walkway grass began to green up and the first probes of Mr. Wrobel's rhubarb and Agnes's flowers penetrated the earth's surface. I tested the soil with my rake and reported to Adam, watching from his bedroom window, that the ground wasn't the least bit frozen. It had a calloused skin, but was soft and dark underneath and, when stirred by my rake, gave up a thick, loamy fragrance. As Adam watched, I flipped the urn over the expanse of mud that in a few month would be lush with new tomato plants. Out came hunks of ash, then a gray powder, and finally a white smoke. I raked the remains into the soil, leaned on my rake and, looking up at Adam, waved forlornly to him. Then I went to get the mail.

That summer, I planted and assiduously cared for the tomatoes (I chose Big Boys, her favorites), fertilizing them once a week as Agnes had done. By August, they were ready to eat, but you know what? We couldn't eat them. It made us too sad. I called the Goodworks Shelter and they sent a young woman named Ann to harvest the crop for their soup kitchen. She was unusually tall with flowing ginger-brown hair, thin lips, a pianist's fingers, and a lovely smile. She was beautiful, but her beauty was a kind of radiance, stemming from her simple reserve and genuine kindness. Adam, whom I saw staring out of his window, couldn't take his eyes off her the whole time she was in the backyard picking tomatoes. No doubt she had heard about the hermit of 7 Peru Street, but she didn't say anything nor did she ask any questions. Adam said he would have liked to talk with her. Through the door, of course.

6

LATER IN THE YEAR, MR. TERRENCE CALLED ME on the phone and said he had never stopped thinking about Pie Man Pies and about Agnes, who had so impressed him and whose death seemed more and more tragic as time went on. He said he wanted to negotiate a partnership arrangement that would make Shop&Save the exclusive distributor of a resurrected Pie Man Pies. I wondered if by *arrangement* he actually meant *buyout* and, sure enough, Mr. Terrence admitted that that was where the partnership would ultimately end up. He was happy that I had, to use his words, cut to the chase. All I had to do was name our price and the real negotiations could begin.

"There's one problem," I said. "I don't know anything about how Agnes made her pies. Only Danuta does. She and Agnes ran the operation, with Anna and Zosia as their assistants."

"Then Danuta probably should be production manager and the other two should continue as her assistants," Mr. Terrence said. "Actually we have plans for a new Pie Man Pies plant to be located here in Silverton. We were thinking of moving the ovens at the old bakery on Bolivia Street to the abandoned chocolate factory on Locust. Pie Man Pies would be made there, a little farther away from you, but still part of Agnes's neighborhood, so to speak."

The buyout, continued Mr. Terrence, would not only include the recipes and such, but full ownership of and a generous settlement for the Pie Man Pies name and the Pie Man logo which, he promised, would become a common sight around town and eventually throughout the Northeast.

I said I would like to think about it, that is, discuss it with Adam. Mr. Terrence said he understood. That evening, Adam and I talked it over. He was all for the sale. It was, he said, Agnes's legacy. He also agreed with me that Danuta should be given a managerial job in the new company, if she wanted it, of course, and that the girls be hired as her assistants. I also talked to the attorney who advised us for Pie

Man Pies and he said, as far as he could tell (he would have to see the contract first, of course), it sounded like a good deal. We had nothing to lose. The next day I called Mr. Terrence and gave him our price. Adam and I later thought we had probably asked too little because he accepted our figure without hesitation.

7

IN A MATTER OF MONTHS, DANUTA AND THE sisters were working five blocks away at the new Pie Man Pies plant on Locust Street making Pie Man Pies. Were they as good as Agnes's? No, but they were good and they sold at a reasonable price and seemed to be getting off to a great start.

At 7 Peru Street, Adam and I continued our new routine, one without Agnes, without pies, without the chaos and noise. During the day, the house belonged entirely to Adam. He told me he ventured out of his room during the daylight hours so long as he was sure no one saw him (the shades were always drawn, the doors always locked). When I got home from the Aircraft or if there were a knock on the front door, he was in his room in record time. Usually, Adam prepared dinner for me, leaving it warming in the oven. I ate, then went upstairs to chat with Adam through the door. He had become an excellent cook; the only thing he never ventured to make was pie of any kind.

During the day, Adam said, the house was eerily quiet. All he heard was his breathing, his footsteps, the house's inveterate noises. Every other month or so, Danuta and Alfredo (now Lt. Fiore) came over for dinner. Adam prepared the meal but never joined us. Our friends usually brought with them wine and new Pie Man Pies. In them Adam and I recognized the delicate sweetness and some of the nuances of Agnes's creations: no surprise, since Danuta continued to use Agnes's recipes and baking secrets. Adam had even seen a Pie Man Pies commercial on the television, a ballet of bakers wearing unsullied white aprons and puffy toques.

8

DAY FOLLOWED DAY FOLLOWED DAY AND SINCE one day was nearly exactly like the one before and the one after, the passing months and then years seemed to melt away, collecting and coagulating into a single composite day. Time, which had always been meaningless to Adam, had also become insubstantial, no longer a medium of existence or a measurement of activity. The hand of the clock moved, calendar leaves blew off into space as in the movies, but at the end of it all, twenty years seemed as long as a single day, divisible into morning, afternoon, and night: Adam's unwavering isolation, my retirement, our introduction to the personal computer.

9

AFTER AGNES'S DEATH, ADAM WAS NO LONGER interested in watching over the neighborhood. His vigilance grew lax and occasional. Now and then he found himself sitting in front of his bedroom window, but he was, he said, looking *through* the neighborhood, not *at* it. And it wasn't the same neighborhood anyway. The Glowac family had followed Alex to California, the Rocques were now alone and dogless in their old age, Mrs. Chmura's daughter had married and eventually moved to New Hampshire, Kozak's Market was now a duplex apartment, and the K-Club could barely sustain itself on the few nightly beers of old men whose lives illness had robbed of vitality and death had robbed of fellowship. Adam no longer knew who was who and who lived where anymore. He saw familiar faces but could no longer connect them with houses. Puerto Rican and black faces mixed with white ones, and a host of black boys rode stripped-down bikes up and down Bolivia and Peru Streets, balancing on one wheel or maneuvering in tight, daring figure eights. On summer nights, he heard the young people talking in the park, their stories and theories and harangues carried by the breezes, and he was glad to know that they still talked about him, still made up fantastic stories and, even though he didn't understand much of their slang, it seemed that he had become more of a gothic figure in their tales, a vampire with skin as white and luminescent as the moon.

10

AS FAR AS I COULD TELL, ADAM SPENT MOST OF his time drawing or reading, watching the television (when movies were on), or listening to music. He found it impossible to listen to Chopin or Maurice Ravel because they made him think of his mother and how much he missed her.

The truth was just as Adam said it would be: he and I would never get over missing Agnes. For us, time healed nothing. With Agnes gone, I worked more hours than ever at the Aircraft, and when I was home, I was either chatting with Adam through the door or in my workroom downstairs, building birdhouses or fixing appliances or making repairs on the house.

Adam's new interest in cooking meant that we started eating very well, no more spaghetti sauce from a jar, no more American cheese sandwiches. Adam said that after Agnes died, the world was missing her 120 pounds and he promised that he and I would eventually put it back again. As it turned out, it was Adam who returned those 120 pounds (or so he said). I actually lost weight during those years.

Adam and I continued to enjoy our post-dinner talks. It was, as it had always been, our time together. We talked about the news, about what Adam was reading, about movies, about the latest developments at the Aircraft or the union and, to a lesser and lesser extent, about the house and the neighborhood. And on Friday nights, I came home with pizza from the Little Rendezvous: a medium plain for Adam and a medium sausage and mushroom for myself. Adam never tried to make his own pizza; he didn't explain why. I think it was because the Little Rendezvous pizza was so good or else it had to do with his unspoken vow never to make a pie of any kind.

11

TIRED OF CIGARETTES, ADAM TOOK UP SMOKING a briarwood pipe I had bought for myself (and used only occasionally) when Adam was five or six. He even smoked the same brand of tobacco I once did: Middleton Cherry. Adam also took up drinking and a day didn't pass when he didn't have a vodka at four, a glass of wine or two with his dinner, and a cordial, usually blackberry brandy, at night. In time, a liquor store on Canada Street, owned by a friend of Witold's known as Benjamin the Banker, started making monthly deliveries to 7 Peru Street. Once in a while, Adam drank too much, but he never did anything uncharacteristic, never made a fool of himself, and never allowed me, and certainly not anyone else, to look at him.

12

FOR NEARLY ALL OF HIS LIFE, ADAM HAD ENJOYED drawing and painting. His favorite subjects had been his neighbors and his beloved house (an architectural detail or flourish, that sort of thing), but now he seemed more interested in what the house happened to contain at the moment: his pipe, a bowl of soup, a sandwich, a pouch of Middleton Cherry tobacco, a pencil, my lunch pail, my Sunday sausage, and so on.

To some extent, his drawing style remained the same (a meticulous, near-photographic accuracy), but as he got older, he added another step. After he finished a drawing, he deliberately sabotaged what he had drawn, turning what had been so precise into something appearing sloppy and carefree through erasing, rubbing, scribbling, and smearing. The thing drawn now had its own face, its own life. A few works he gave away to Dr. Cohen or Danuta, but nearly all of them stayed in the room where they were conceived, until he piled them up in the hallway, and I did what Agnes had done for so many years, placed them in portfolios in chronological order, and then stacked them on shelves in the living room, shelves I had built so long ago.

13

IN 1990, AT THE AGE OF SIXTY-FIVE, I RETIRED from the Aircraft. My managers had asked me to continue on at a substantial increase in salary, but I refused any kind of full-time employment. I wanted to spend more time at home with my son, hoping that my daily presence would allow him to put an end to his isolation. Maybe, I thought, he would be able to tolerate being with me and being seen by me and we could go about a day's business and enjoy each other's company.

In the end, I accepted a generous offer to work as a consultant, coming into the plant once a month or so to discuss technical matters with the master mechanic who replaced me and whom I had trained for nearly ten years. It was barely work at all. I was, practically speaking, retired, but it really didn't make that much of a difference when it came to my relationship with Adam.

From the first day of my retirement, Adam and I had every opportunity to spend time together, to be friends, to be father and son, but we didn't take advantage of it. We didn't watch television together, we didn't eat together, we didn't read the newspaper together. He drew or painted countless portraits of me in his first-neat-then-roughed-up style, but I never actually sat for him. He left his room, but never in my presence. We became expert at avoiding each other.

14

IN 1993, I BOUGHT A PERSONAL COMPUTER, WHICH I used for writing letters, keeping track of expenses, and keeping tabs on my pension, savings, investments, and our Shop&Save money. Adam expressed no interest in the computer and thought it was no more than an elaborate electronic toy. It was only later, with the emergence of the internet, that he became curious and sought out my help, through his bedroom door, of course. Soon, he was communicating with dozens of people around the world and, in many cases, befriending them, chatting with them about politics or books or current events. When I say friends, I mean friends of a kind, not flesh-and-blood friends, like Miss T. or Danuta, but friends made out of words and that, as far as it went, was fine by Adam. But the internet also unleashed armies of ignorant and closed-minded fools who invaded his privacy and defiled his sense of courtesy

For a time, Adam became something of a celebrity among his internet friends. To them he was a shadowy, solitary figure, an honest-to-goodness recluse, a man who couldn't or wouldn't leave his house and who avoided contact with people, even those closest to him, namely me. They were always reverent in their communications, deferential, as if he were a holy man. He even received an offer of marriage, which he refused, and wordy compliments, which he accepted with a simple thank you. They saw him as a more rarified version of themselves, the pure and eternal student, untainted by a profession, by the marketplace, by the world's endless imperfections and compromises. He refused to create his own web site (even though I was willing to build and manage it) and was disheartened to learn that others had created one for him, without his knowledge and against his wishes, collecting his opinions and comments along with a photograph of the house at 7 Peru Street, which Adam didn't authorize. He also refused to send them any of his drawings, paintings, or sketches. Adam was embarrassed by his new fame, modest though it was, and tried not to pay any attention to it.

Eventually he became bored by it all, dramatically limited his time on the web and reduced his so-called friends to a handful, a solid core. In time his website was dismantled. By then he was using the internet solely for educational purposes. He signed up for online courses that appealed to him (his only criterion), and it seemed that, in spirit at least, Miss T. had returned once again to 7 Peru Street. Over time, he earned four degrees. Or maybe it was five.

15

ONE MIGHT THINK THAT ADAM AND I WOULD have bumped into each other now and then, but that never happened. Adam wandered the house and backyard, but only at night, when I was asleep. When I was working at the Aircraft, Adam used to make dinner for me. After my retirement, Adam continued making dinners but insisted that I leave the house each day around four-thirty and walk down to the K-Club and have a beer with my friends. When I came back, dinner was waiting for me and Adam was nowhere to be seen (we ate at the same time, just in different rooms).

There were times when I'd catch glimpses of him, but he was only a blur passing from room to room or streaking up the stairs. I never saw his face, although I could tell from what I did see that his hair was very long, hanging down below his shoulders, and some of it was turning gray. I couldn't tell if he wore a beard or mustache. I assumed he did because I never bought him razor blades or shaving cream when I went shopping.

16

I DON'T THINK A DAY EVER PASSED WHEN EITHER Adam or I didn't mention Agnes's name. One time we talked at length about her pre-PMP self, when she used to make pies for neighbors who were sick or had suffered some kind of loss. Adam suggested that he and I ought to continue that tradition. We couldn't make pies, of course, but we could set up a fund with our Shop&Save money that would help people in the neighborhood meet crises in their lives: pay outstanding bills, or settle a debt, or send children to college, or pay for a special operation or a prohibitively expensive medicine, or even meet funeral expenses. The Agnes Fund, as we called it, would be managed by the Goodworks Shelter with (Adam insisted) the lovely young Ann as our liaison and fund manager. Adam and I agreed on a few stipulations. The money could not be reinvested by the Shelter, that is, it couldn't function as an endowment. It was to be spent, immediately and directly, on those neighbors who needed financial assistance to get through a rough time. Adam also insisted there be no red tape. No application forms, no interviews. The Shelter staff members had to discover for themselves who needed help. They had to be aware of what was going on in the neighborhood exactly as Adam had when he was younger. The Fund was Adam-like in another way. It was secret. No one could know about the Fund or our involvement in it or even the Shelter's involvement, and the people in need didn't even have to contact the Shelter. In fact, they didn't have to do anything. The Shelter just mailed them a check. The money would be a complete surprise and a complete mystery.

The next day Ann arrived at our door and sat down with me in the parlor. We had tea. She was a delightful young woman, and I could see why Adam flipped over her when she had come by for Agnes's tomatoes. It occurred to me that Adam, listening to her from the top of the stairs, would no doubt give every cent we owned to the Shelter just to hear her voice.

17

A FEW DAYS AFTER MY SEVENTIETH BIRTHDAY, I had dinner with my friend Witold at a new restaurant on the turnpike. I remember we had apple pie for dessert, but they served it in a pool of warmed honey. Witold said he liked the idea of it, being the son of a beekeeper, but the pie didn't compare to anything Agnes made.

I came home and watched the television, sipping on some honey liqueur I kept in the house for reasons I had long forgotten. Eating the honey-saturated pie had awakened my sweet tooth, I suppose, and I craved the liqueur's cloying and comforting thickness.

After a while, I went upstairs to bed. I stopped in front of Adam's door and placed my ear to it thinking he might be up listening to music or watching the television, but it was perfectly quiet. I assumed he was asleep. I always assumed his door was locked, but for some inexplicable reason, I tried it anyway. It swung open. And there in front of me was Adam's room in all its obsessively neat splendor. It looked like a section of the town library; every wall was filled with books. And there was his television, his short wave, his drawing table, his green chair (in good shape after all those years), his standup ashtray (the brasswork still shiny), and drawings and paintings on every available space not taken up by book shelving, including the original "self-portrait" he had done as a boy and which Agnieszka had used as the basis for her PMP logo.

I stood in the doorway, probably with my mouth open. I hadn't seen the inside of this room for decades. It was amazing how clean it was, how ordered. One of the problems Agnes had with Adam locking himself in his room was that she couldn't clean it. But it turned out that the son was as fastidious as the mother. I had a dream once, in which Adam's door opened and revealed a room stacked so high with books and magazines and papers and junk that one could no longer breathe in it. The dream was, of course, a reflection of my workshop rather than Adam's room.

Then it occurred to me (genius that I am!) that Adam wasn't there.

I searched Adam's room more closely, then went into the bathroom (immaculate: no germ could live there). Finally, I returned to the corridor and made my way to my bedroom. When I turned on the light I saw something I hadn't seen in over thirty years: I saw my son's face. He was sleeping in my bed, sleeping as peacefully as a baby. He had, as I'd suspected from my brief glimpses of him over the years, gained a great deal of weight, probably more than the 120 pounds Agnes had taken with her. He was forty-five years old. His hair was shoulder-length and graying; his beard was full and neatly trimmed and also graying. He was sad-eyed and unhealthy-looking and, since he hadn't been out in the sun in decades, his skin was waxy and albino-pale.

Oh, but it was so wonderful to look at him again, to study his features, to watch his chest move up and down as he breathed, to see the jittery movement of his eyes behind his eyelids. He was a handsome man despite his puffiness and pallor. I couldn't get enough of looking at him. I stared and stared and stared. The greatest tragedy I could imagine had brought me the greatest joy I'd ever experienced.

Eventually, I crawled into bed with him. He must have sensed my presence because he grunted ever so slightly. I tried to sleep but couldn't. I couldn't stop looking at him, imagining what Agnes would have said had she been the one staring at him. Tough and resilient as she was, she still wouldn't have been able to hold back tears. Soon I began to sob. Who wouldn't in my position? But then all the old questions and doubts returned. Had we done the right thing? Should we have yanked him into the world after all?

Then Adam snorted. He rolled over and draped his arm across my chest, something Hardy might do to Laurel in an old movie. I didn't dare move. I barely breathed. And then I fell asleep.

18

I THOUGHT FROM THAT DAY ON THAT ADAM AND I would share what remained of our lives. We would watch the television together, eat together, listen to music together, and so on and so forth. But that didn't happen. Adam announced that he had, in part, gained control of himself. He was no longer a collection of fears and dire imaginings, no longer the house or the house's agent, at least not in my presence. But that evening, my birthday and our very first dinner together, I could see the agony he was experiencing. He was squirming (and trying to conceal it from me), his mouth was crooked with pain and on the verge of emitting a cry, his eyes were gaping and wet, his nose flared and at one point produced a drop of blood. Finally, he left the table to go upstairs, go to the bathroom, he said, but I knew better. He had managed to leave his room, maybe as a birthday present for me, but couldn't sustain the effort. My eyes must have been like little lasers to him. But even though this was another failed experiment, no less noble than the time I tried to drive him to freedom in the family car, I was still positively rapturous at being able to look at him and talk to him even for that short a time.

Life went on at 7 Peru Street as before. Adam still pretty much avoided me, although sometimes he sat with me for dinner, excruciating an experience though it was, and once in a while he'd come into the den when I was watching a movie on the television, and he'd sit with me, explaining subtleties, providing insights into the symbolism or cinematic technique, that sort of thing. Of course, if Danuta or Dr. Cohen or anyone else (even the lovely Ann) came to the house, he vanished into his room. The only eyes that could look at him were mine and only for short periods of time. But every day, he said, no doubt to mollify me, the pain was gradually diminishing.

In the warmer months, Adam continued to sit outside smoking and doing who knows what. When the Glowac's sprawling oak finally came down, rotten to the core, he suddenly had an open look at the night sky. For his fiftieth birthday, I bought him a telescope that he soon couldn't live without. Instead of staying outside for an hour or so, he spent, on clear nights at least, three or four or even five hours in the backyard. Even on the coldest night, there he was, dressed in a parka and Russian hat, turning knobs with gloved hands, eavesdropping on the stars. His life was suddenly turned inside out. He became a bona fide nocturnal creature. This meant that we saw even less of each other. When he was up looking at the heavens, I was in bed snoring away. When I was up and about, fixing things or reading or taking my constitutional or having a beer at the K-Club, he was asleep in his room. We did sometimes meet briefly at the dinner table or in the den, and I noticed he was becoming less and less nervous, not so stressed. He was more comfortable in my presence. He laughed more, teased me affectionately, called me Mr. Fixit. I sensed that maybe he was really changing. Maybe the pain we others inflicted on him was growing impotent. Or maybe he was just realizing that his fears had all along been silly and tragic and had conspired to ruin his life.

19

ONE AFTERNOON, ADAM WOKE UP AND CAME downstairs to help me make dinner. He said he had had a strange and vivid dream. In this dream, a crowd of fifty or so people gathered on the walkway. He said he recognized a number of his neighbors, the Sylvesters from Maine, the Pereyos who lived in the former Glowac house, the Perez family who lived in the old Chmura house on the corner, and Mr. and Mrs. Rocque, frail and wide eyed. But the others were only vaguely familiar, faces he might have seen from his bedroom window, sturdy t-shirted men who worked in construction or in factories, young children who hid behind their mother's skirts, and the older daredevils who rode their stripped-down bikes along Peru and Bolivia Streets. They pointed at his bedroom window and called him Pie Man and hermit and said he was a saint, touched by God. One old man said Adam was from outer space, begoggled, chalk-white. The next instant Adam was outside, in his backyard. He took a step toward the crowd and they, in response, took a step back. Only some of the older boys, eager to see the man who had been the subject of countless stories and jokes and imagined sightings, remained where they were, hanging on to the fence that held the cucumber vines, shouting out to Adam, asking him to speak to them, impart some wisdom and shake their extended hands. The crowd was like a swelling body of water, ready to drown him. Hands were in Adam's face, hands tugged at his beard, hands messed his hair. But he wasn't afraid. In fact, he smiled. He walked into the sea of his neighbors and grabbed each hand and held it for a second or two, saying hello, hello, hello, asking what their names were and where they lived, telling them his name was Adam Olszewski and saying yes, yes, yes, he was the hermit, he was Pie Man and he never left his house. He shook hands with some of the boys who, even now, left candy at his door on Halloween. He met their fathers who saluted him and patted him on the shoulder and took his pale soft hand into theirs, and he met their mothers and grandmothers, many of whom looked tired and cynical. Some of them worked at the Pie Man Pies plant and showed Adam their ID badges. The crowd pushed against the cucumber fence until it gave way and lay flat on the mint plants, still pungent, which I had planted years before to replace Agnes's tomatoes.

"*Ermitaño!*" they cried. "Pie Man!"

A few women, looking crazed and jittery, wanted to touch his shirt, as if he were an object of good luck. Then many of those who had been standing on Peru Street came into the walkway to get a closer look and there was a great buzz, in English and in Spanish and now and then in Polish. Who were these people? Eventually, the talking stopped and the interest in Adam subsided. He was just one of them, one of the crowd, chatting about the inconsequential, ordinary things that good neighbors chat about.

20

THE YEARS PASSED. LITTLE CHANGED. ADAM lived his nocturnal life, I lived my diurnal life, and we tried our best to meet in the middle. Adam was always cheerful and positive, but sitting with him at the dinner table or watching television with him, a grown man in his fifties, was sometimes painful for me. I couldn't help seeing the potential he had and how it had all gone to waste. He had become nothing. He had grown, but he hadn't grown up. He hadn't made a mark in the world. He was, I thought in my heart of hearts, a failure at life.

How could I have allowed this to happen? How could a life have been shaped by an idea or fear or whatever it was that germinated in the mind of a seven-year-old boy? How could it have sustained itself for all those years? And yet it had. It was still an active idea and Adam still accepted it and lived by it. Moreover, it had given him permission to settle into what could be called a comfortable life, to achieve a kind of happiness, a kind of contentment. Maybe I was fooling myself, but I often wondered if anyone else's life was, in essence, any different from his. Didn't we all discard our talents? Waste part of our lives? Weren't we all prisoners of some kind? Didn't we all, even the most successful of us, fail in some way? And didn't the biggest failures among us succeed in some way?

I could never be critical of Adam for very long. I was as forgiving of him as Agnes had been. After all, what had I done with my life? What gave a man who'd spent year after year in a dark, foul-smelling factory (in August the men's sweat would actually form clouds in the rafters) the right to criticize? My mark on the world was barely a scratch. I wondered if Adam thought that about me, thought I hadn't lived up to *my* potential. I'm sure he did. His was not, I think, an unexamined life. I'm sure he spent hours and hours mulling over what might have been had the circumstances (and he) been different. I once asked him if he had any regrets. It was an innocent question. Everyone had regrets, why not Adam? But he only shrugged his shoulders. We lived a comfortable life, he said. We loved each other. We were healthy. We helped our neighbors. We had the memory of Agnes to cherish. It was, he said without saying so, a ridiculous question.

21

ON A LOVELY MAY DAY, I WENT TO TAKE A PISS and when I did a wine-red liquid flowed out of me and along with it dark clots of blood that, once they struck the toilet water and burst open, took the shape of little red bats. I braced myself against the bathroom wall and called out for help. I was dizzy and nauseous and could barely keep my feet. Adam came running down the stairs, listened to my panicked assessment of the situation and, realizing I was in no shape to drive, called for an ambulance. He helped me to the sofa in the den and made sure I was comfortable. Then he wrote a note for the emergency crew, explaining what had happened and informing them where I was, and he taped it to the front door (which he made sure was unlocked). He called Dr. Cohen and left a message for him with his office. He sat on the sofa with me, and when he heard the ambulance he rushed upstairs and vanished from sight. When Dr. Cohen brought me back several hours later, Adam was in his room, the door locked. When he was certain Dr. Cohen had left, he called out to me and, in his old spot behind the door, asked me question after question until he was satisfied he knew I was all right. It turned out I had bladder cancer, a superficial form of it. Polyps had formed along the bladder's inner wall and these would have to be removed, kind of like scraping little mud wasp nests off the side of the house.

After he drove me home, Dr. Cohen and I spent an hour or so reminiscing. We talked about our film of Adam, about the various stages of his isolation and, of course, we talked about Agnes: what a pip she was, how upset she could get about things, how obsessive and intense, too, sometimes. He said he had eaten one of those new Pie Man Pies, and he admitted it was good, but no match for Agnes's. He said he lived for Agnes's pies and whenever he made a house call or dropped by when he was in the neighborhood, he expected a healthy slice or two or even three: and Agnes never disappointed. I told him I had nightly urges to reach into my fridge at home and pull out one of

Agnes's lemon meringues or coconut custards or French apples with that nice thick vanilla icing. And so there we were, two old men sitting in the kitchen drooling over my late wife's pies.

22

MY KNOWLEDGE AND UNDERSTANDING OF Adam's life wasn't filled with gaps—it was one big gap. So now and then I asked him about this and that, about what he did all day and night in his room, what he thought about me, his mother, Pie Man Pies, the neighborhood, life in general. He answered dutifully but never expansively. It was enough for him to list his daily activities, express his love for Agnes and me and his affection for the girls who worked at 7 Peru Street, particularly Betsy and, which surprised me, the dreamy, goofy Wanda.

He also tried to clear up any misconceptions I might have had. Yes, he did have a crush on Angela Wrobel that extended from boyhood to manhood, but the person he was most fond of, next to Agnes and me, of course, was Miss T. She was the biggest influence in his life. Whatever curiosity he had about the neighborhood and the world came from her. She taught him enthusiasm and gave him a hunger for knowledge. She, he said, was the one he truly loved.

He also corrected me one day when I said he had been pretty lucky over the years to have remained healthy and have kept Dr. Cohen at bay. I said it was because he was living in a vacuum, practically speaking, never in contact with people and their germs. I was very much surprised when he told me that that wasn't the case. He said he was quite frequently sick, not with only the usual colds and sniffles, but with severe chest pains and chills that made him tremble. Scariest of all were the heart palpitations. Sometimes it seemed as if his heart were going to jump out of his chest. Of course, he never said anything about his pains and discomforts, not to Agnes, nor me, nor his cherished Miss T. He just kept quiet, which accounted for those extra-long periods of silence. We thought he was being moody and sullen, but he was silent because he didn't want to give himself away, to give us clues, a croaky or quivery voice or stuffed nose. He'd wait for the illness to pass, for the palpitations and throbbing arrhythmias to calm down. And, he confessed, the times, most recently, when he didn't leave his room for days on end had nothing to do with his need for solitude: he was sick and didn't want me to know about it.

23

THE HOURS ADAM AND I SPENT TOGETHER didn't add up to very many, but they were enough to keep a kind of balance in the house. If I saw Adam for ten or fifteen minutes a day, I was happy. It was still a joy to see him and hear his beautiful voice. When we were together we had a great old time chatting and joking and teasing each other. Sometimes at dinner we ate a bit too much and sometimes, after dinner, we drank too much, but we had fun doing it. I can't remember a day when Adam seemed depressed or in a bad mood. He was always cheerful with me. He did his share of the chores, and he sometimes used my workshop to fix something (usually late at night when I was asleep). He gazed at the stars whenever the weather allowed. He had a mischievous grin and it seemed to me that that teasing, affectionate smirk defined his face and his personality: something I couldn't see behind a closed door.

24

I LOVED ADAM SINCE THE DAY HE WAS BORN, BUT it wasn't until he left his room that our love for each other became visible, the way it was when Adam was a little boy, posited on the world for all the world to see if, that is, the world were allowed to see it.

25

ONE DAY HE SAID HE WAS DETERMINED TO GO beyond the house's dominion, to take walks up and down Peru Street. I don't know why. When I asked him directly, he said he wanted to explore the world and then smiled in such a way that I knew he was pulling my leg. Still, he was determined and extremely patient. It took him weeks and weeks just to get a few yards outside the front door. I remember seeing him at first light from my bedroom window. He'd leave the house, take a few steps, and return inside, repeating this ten or so times before coming inside to stay. He did this every morning at around four o'clock. At first, he seemed to be acting like a laboratory rat, going back and forth, back and forth, for no apparent reason; but he told me that each time he did this little dance of his he went an inch or two farther. After several weeks, he reached the Peru Street sidewalk and he continued, inch by inch, toward the park. One day, he reported with great excitement that he had passed people during his morning constitutional, and while he averted his eyes and pulled down his beat-up felt fedora, which he wore on these occasions, to touch the tip of his nose, he managed to say good morning and pass them by with only minimal discomfort.

By the next year, Adam was walking along Peru Street all the way to the park entrance or, in another direction, over to Bolivia Street and the duplex that once was Kozak's Market, or, in a third direction, to just beyond the corner of Mexico and Peru. There was only one restriction to his new freedom: he had to keep our house within view. If he took a few steps down Mexico Street and could no longer see 7 Peru Street because the Perez house was in the way, he'd feel a sharp stinging in his chest, he'd tremble violently, and his throat would start to constrict. If he continued in that way, he said, he would lose consciousness, maybe for good.

If he took his walk early enough, he'd see a few people on their way to work at the Pie Man Pies plant on Locust Street. Danuta was still the manager there, the Big Boss, Alfredo called her, overseeing the work of twenty or thirty people, including Anna Maria and Zosia, her trusted assistants. The sisters were now married and had children, all of them shamelessly spoiled by Danuta, who had decided against having kids of her own.

Sometimes Adam saw a Pie Man Pies truck rattle down Bolivia Street, dazzling white in the early morning light, adorned with Adam's red boyhood pieface and crammed with pies fresh out of the ovens. Sometimes, when there was a strong breeze from the south, he could smell the pies baking. Most times, though, the only thing he smelled was the burnt toast of hasty breakfasts in the houses he passed.

Sometimes he heard a few distant words in Spanish or lively music coming from tiny transistor radios like shrill, frantic whispering and, once in a while, someone said hello to him, Pie Man, and asked him how he was doing.

By then few if any of his neighbors thought of him as a prisoner or monster. It was plain to see he could now walk the streets a free man, a neighbor like everyone else. He had progressed from a few steps beyond the threshold of his kitchen door to almost the entire length of Peru Street, and there was no reason why he couldn't go a little farther each day. He thought maybe he could go beyond the house's sphere, to walk without keeping 7 Peru Street in view, go beyond the park gate, all the way to Canada Street, past the bus stop, and maybe even downtown. He could go the length of Mexico Street, down to Jefferson or up to Burma. He could go a little farther every day: an inch today, an inch tomorrow.

26

ON A SEPTEMBER MORNING IN 2010, I WENT downstairs to have breakfast, expecting to find Adam back from his predawn walk, sitting at the kitchen table reading the newspaper. But the kitchen was cold, the table was empty, the coffee hadn't been made, the paper was still at the front door. I retraced my steps, went upstairs and knocked on Adam's door. When there was no answer, I stepped in and saw Adam in his bed, blankets under his chin, his eyes closed, his face ashen. I touched his forehead and it was cold. I felt a tremor under my feet as if the house had just shuddered, as if it knew that the person it loved and was connected to was no more. The house shuddered a second time and I had to grab the bedpost to keep my balance.

I uncovered the blankets and slipped into bed with my son. I inched up against his body; his skin was cold and almost brittle, not at all resilient like living tissue. I started to weep, a confusion of streams and rivers flowing this way and that; but, next to me, nothing flowed. Everything there had settled into inert pools.

I fell asleep sharing Adam's pillow. When I woke up I heard the radiators clanking. I listened more closely, hoping that I might hear some kind of house-eulogy. Of course, I heard nothing. I got out of bed and called the hospital. An ambulance arrived a short while later. A few solemn young men went upstairs to fetch the body. Later, the youngest of them shook his head at me. He said it was most likely that Adam's heart had given out. I nodded: maybe all those years of smoking and sedentariness and, more recently, of drinking and eating to excess, had done him in.

After the ambulance took Adam away, carrying him into the world for the first time in more than fifty years, Danuta came by. I was sitting at the kitchen table, my face slippery from tears. I barely had enough strength to stand up and greet her. Danuta made coffee and the two of us sat at the kitchen table talking about the funeral arrangements. Adam wanted his body to be cremated, like Agnes's, but the ashes were not to be raked into the garden soil. They would remain in the urn and the urn would remain in the house: it didn't matter what room so long as the urn never left the house. As for a wake or reception, I said I was certainly against having one at a funeral home or church, and I didn't think it should be anything like what we had had for Agnes. Agnes was a public person, she had turned the house into a bustling, hectic workplace, so it made sense to have people come to our house to pay their respects. But Adam was the most private of individuals. He would never have wanted us to make a fuss. Maybe a quiet vigil would be right, I said, maybe something as simple and dignified as a moment of silence.

"I mean, how many people would come to a hermit's funeral anyway?" I asked with a little sarcastic laugh.

"I bet more than you'd think," Danuta replied. "I don't think a reception at the K-Club would be right, but maybe you should just open your house."

"To whom?"

"You'll see."

27

A FEW DAYS LATER, AT TEN IN THE MORNING, people started arriving at 7 Peru Street. Many of them I recognized from Agnes's funeral, including Mr. Terrence, and many I had known for decades—Witold, the Kozaks, my Aircraft friends, and old K-Club buddies among them. But most of the people I didn't know. Some I'd seen in the neighborhood or in the park, some were complete strangers to me. I invited every one of them inside for coffee or something stronger (Alfredo had set up a little bar in the dining room and was kind enough to volunteer as bartender). Danuta suggested that we also serve pie in honor of Agnes, and she brought a carload of pies from the Pie Man Pies plant. This turned out to be a mistake, but a very funny one, because the people who came over to pay their respects—nearly every one of them, even the total strangers—also brought Pie Man Pies with them. The house, as Witold put it, "was crawling with pies." There must have been a hundred of them, maybe more. People came to the door, shook my hand or embraced me, then gave me a pie. To them Adam was Pie Man and what better gift to bring than a Pie Man Pie? I tried to explain that that wasn't really the case, that Adam really had nothing to do with Pie Man Pies (except for his boyhood image on the packaging and trucks), that it was entirely his mother's concern, but I soon gave up. It just didn't matter.

We stacked the pies in the kitchen and for a brief second it seemed as if Pie Man Pies were still being made in our house. I could easily mistake the funereal chatter for the Polish girls' chit chat and could almost see Agnes, dusted with flour, cutting apples or stirring the filling as it bubbled away on the stove.

The question remained, however: what were we going to do with all those pies? It was a question that cheered us up because it was so ridiculous. In fact, when Wanda, tipsy when she arrived, came into the kitchen looking for her Paul, she laughed out loud at the number of pie boxes. Danuta suggested we only had one course: accept the pies people brought, serve them pie and coffee and whatever, then give them two pies when they left. We came up a few pies short, but that was fine.

28

THE NEXT DAY I RECEIVED A CARD FROM YOUNG Alex. In it he wrote simply:

> Mr. O., I'm so very sorry. The world won't miss him because the world didn't know him. It's the world's loss. Those of us who knew him and loved him will miss him for the rest of our days. Alex.

That same day I received a letter from Miss T. in Florida.

> I would have written to you sooner—except that I've been crying my eyes out these past few days. I would have called you. I would have done this and that. I would have done a million things. But I don't know what to do with myself anymore. I live in my fancy-pants cabaña—it's not really that, it's like twenty cabañas piled one on top of the other—and I have people waiting on me—making me meals and serving me drinks and forcing pills down my throat—and I still don't know which end is up or if I'm coming or going. I would have done the right thing and come up north to see you and give you a big hug—but I don't leave my house much anymore. I don't need to, I have everything I need here—I have people doing everything for me. I've become a hermit just like Adam, except I'm not afraid of people—I'm disgusted by them, by how stupid and petty and greedy they are, by how ugly they are, even the most handsome or beautiful. I don't lock myself in my house. I go out on drives—I can still drive!—but I don't go very far from my house. I mostly go to the beach a few blocks away—when it's

not too hot and the bugs aren't too bad I'll walk, take my constitutional—and I go to a little private beach and sit on a park bench and watch the ocean come in and go out—and I'll stay there all day! That's really what I like to do. Even more than listen to music, which I do very little of anymore—and I don't play at all, not a note—and sometimes I've come to hate music—just hate it! It's the ocean I love now, really love—in and out—in and out—because there at the beach I can be a hermit like Adam and still be right in the middle of a crowd of people—horrible disgusting people, fat awful people, stupid greedy awful people—but I can tune them out—everyone and everything—and that, sadly, is what Adam never really learned to do. He could have gone out into the world and stayed in his room *at the same time*—not an easy trick, I suppose, but I won't say he couldn't do it, he could do anything he wanted—instead I think he just didn't want to do it—for whatever reason. But O, my most amazing and lovely Mr. O., to drive to the airport and hop on a plane to Hartford—not a chance. I'm collapsing in on myself, you know, imploding—the way people with explosives—implosives?—take down a building—kaboom—and the thing collapses from within—without making the least bit of a mess. Kaboom kaboom yadadadadadadadadada life could be a dream, sweetheart. XOXOXOXOXOXOX Miss T., the Hermette of West Palm Beach.

29

WITH ADAM GONE, I BECAME ACUTELY AWARE that I would, for the first time in my life, be alone in the world, and I worried that I might find that unsettling, but I soon recognized (as Adam must have years and years ago) that loneliness is like a shirt or sweater, something to put on every day, something ordinary and mindlessly worn and not worthy of more than a moment's thought. But it was there nonetheless, the emptiness, the panic, the foreign, misplaced quality of my voice when I spoke out loud, to myself or to the cat I had adopted as a pet. And now I called loneliness by another name, *solitude*, a less desperate word, a word connoting inner peace and meditation, maybe even wisdom.

It was a week or so later when I started going through Adam's things, mostly for something to do. I thought he might have kept a diary or written some autobiographical pieces, but he hadn't. His last drawing was a portrait (from memory) of his mother.

For weeks and weeks neighbors knocked at the front door to see how I was doing and if I needed anything. Some came by to bring food. The idea was that I, still grieving, had neither the time nor the inclination to cook for myself. They brought casseroles or cookies or lovely flans, but this time not a single pie.

30

AT AROUND FOUR O'CLOCK ONE SEPTEMBER morning, I was in bed thinking that this was the time of day when Adam usually went on his walk. Each time he went out he would try to expand the house's dominion by an inch or two, sometimes even a foot. It had been nearly a year since his heart betrayed him and I found him lifeless in his bed.

I got up. It was unseasonably warm and a pleasant breeze rushed through the open window. I decided I would retrace Adam's steps that morning, maybe learn something about my son and something about the neighborhood, too. The first thing I noticed was how quiet it was and how dim the light was at that time of day. It really wasn't light at all, but a milky kind of darkness. A sliver of a moon hung over downtown like a smile, as if Adam himself were watching over the city, watching over me. Nearly everyone was asleep, including the dogs, and those that were awake didn't bark at me: maybe they had, even after nearly a year's hiatus, become used to someone shuffling up and down the sidewalk so early in the morning. In a couple of hours, the neighborhood children would be clutching desperately to the last vestiges of sleep before being nagged out of bed and sent off to school. After his constitutionals, Adam used to watch them from his green chair as they hopped and skipped down Bolivia Street toward St. Paul in Chains School or continued down to Canada Street to meet the bus for Harriet Beecher Stowe School.

I walked down Peru Street as far as Adam could have gone, the entrance to the park, keeping our house in sight all the while, just as he had. This was where he'd turn around, so I carefully did the same, an about face, but in slow motion. I returned up Peru Street, passing the hedges where Mrs. Wrobel died, then the Rocque house on my right, dark and still from the isolation that old age, as I had discovered for myself, requires and relishes. Then, on my left, there it was again: 7 Peru Street, the beacon Adam couldn't ignore or turn away from.

I reached the Perez house at the end of Peru with its great shagbark hickory, grown more magnificent over the years, even though the power company had trimmed its limbs and ruined some of its symmetry and grace. I turned down Mexico, then walked up Mexico, my eyes, like Adam's, never drifting from 7 Peru Street. It was still a handsome house, I thought, in as good a working order as it ever had been, shipshape and built to last.

I turned the corner and was on Peru Street again. I took a left on Bolivia and, once I reached the duplex that had once been Kozak's Market, I turned around. I picked up my pace a bit, pretending that I was on my way to work, a man with somewhere to go and something to do. A few more lights came on in the houses nearby and I thought this was probably the time Adam went inside. And so did I. The house was, as always, dark, and I found my way to the kitchen as a blind man would, with my hand outstretched. Only when I was in the kitchen did I turn on the overhead light. I put on a kettle of water and shoveled seven tablespoons of coffee into the French press, a Christmas gift from Agnes the year before she died (I should have coffee, she joked, at least half as good as her pies).

When the coffee was done, I poured a cup and sat down at the kitchen table and read the newspaper from beginning to end. I checked the kitchen clock: seven-thirty. This was the time Adam went upstairs to watch the neighborhood children walk to school. I did the same, sitting in his green chair. I was a little late. Already the children were outside: boys were teasing girls, girls were telling secrets to each other, and boys and girls both were breaking out of their pairs and trios and running in circles or twisting in pirouettes for no apparent reason. The St. Paul in Chains girls were dressed in red jumpers and white blouses and white ankle socks; the boys were in khakis, white shirts, and red ties. The public school children, on their way to the bus, didn't wear uniforms at all.

Soon, another group of children walked down Peru Street and turned the corner at Bolivia. How full of life they were, how healthy and bright. Everything was ahead of them. There was nothing for them to regret, nothing that could stop them from moving ahead. Even the boy who, as a joke, walked backwards down Peru Street, was moving forward. They were all Adam's wards, I thought, walking where he had walked when he was alive, following in his footsteps. If it were a snowy day they could have actually stepped in his footsteps, made a game of it, laughed at the bigness of his shoe size and exaggerated the length of his gait. I realized that to these children, I had become the white-haired hermit, the mysterious Pie Man, and even after I passed away, I hoped the children would keep us, Adam and me, alive. They'd grow up and tell their children about us and it would go on and on like that, generation after generation. Even when the house became offices and meeting rooms, the property of the Goodworks Shelter, as Adam and I instructed, Pie Man would still haunt the place, haunt the rooms and gardens, haunt the streets and what remained of the walkway, haunt the houses and the night sky itself. Pie Man would never die and would never move away.

John Surowiecki lives and writes in Hebron, Connecticut. He is the author of several poetry books and chapbooks, including *Missing Persons*, *Flies*, and *The Hat City after Men Stopped Wearing Hats*, as well as the play *My Nose and Me*. The recipient of many awards, Surowiecki received his BA in English from the University of Connecticut in 1966 and his MA in 1976. He's worked as a journalist, copywriter, and teacher.